THE WORLD OF ASTRID LINDGREN

KaRLSSON

Flies Again

OXFORD
UNIVERSITY PRESS

Great Clarendon Street, Oxford OX2 6DP
Oxford University Press is a department of the University of Oxford.
It furthers the University's objective of excellence in research, scholarship,
and education by publishing worldwide. Oxford is a registered trade mark of
Oxford University Press in the UK and in certain other countries

Text © Astrid Lindgren 1962, The Astrid Lindgren Company
Illustrations © Mini Grey 2021

Translated from the Swedish by Sarah Death
English translation © Sarah Death 2009

This translation of *Karlsson Flies Again* originally published in Swedish
published by arrangement with The Astrid Lindgren Company

The moral rights of the author, illustrator, and translator have been asserted

First published in 1962 as *Karlsson på taket flyger igen* by Rabén & Sjögren, Sweden
All foreign rights are handled by The Astrid Lindgren Company, Stockholm, Sweden.
For more information, please contact info@astridlindgren.se

First published in Great Britain by Methuen Children's Books Ltd 1977
First published in this edition 2021 by Oxford University Press

Database right Oxford University Press (maker)

British Library Cataloguing in Publication Data

Data available

ISBN: 978-0-19-277626-6

1 3 5 7 9 10 8 6 4 2

Printed in India

Paper used in the production of this book is a natural,
recyclable product made from wood grown in sustainable forests.
The manufacturing process conforms to the environmental
regulations of the country of origin.

KaRLSSON
Flies Again

BY ASTRID LINDGREN
ILLUSTRATED BY MINI GREY
TRANSLATED BY SARAH DEATH

OXFORD
UNIVERSITY PRESS

THE WORLD OF
ASTRID LINDGREN

BOOKS BY ASTRID LINDGREN
ILLUSTRATED BY MINI GREY

CONTENTS

Karlsson on the Roof Flies Again

The world is big, and there are so many houses in it. Big houses and little houses, pretty houses and ugly houses, old houses and new houses. And then there's a tiny little house for Karlsson on the Roof. Karlsson thinks it's the world's best house and just right for the world's best Karlsson. Smidge thinks so, too.

Smidge lives with Mum and Dad and Seb and Sally in a perfectly ordinary house on a perfectly ordinary street in Stockholm, but up on the roof, just behind the chimney, you'll find the little Karlsson house with its sign saying:

You might think it's funny for someone to be living on the roof, but Smidge says:

'What's funny about that? People can live wherever they want, can't they?'

Mum and Dad think people can live wherever they want, as well. But to start with, they didn't think Karlsson existed. Seb and Sally didn't think so either. They didn't want to believe that a fat little man, who had a propeller on his back and could fly, could live up there.

'You're lying, Smidge,' said Seb and Sally. 'Karlsson's just an invention.'

To be on the safe side, Smidge asked Karlsson if he was an invention, but Karlsson said:

'Invention themselves!'

Mum and Dad had the idea Karlsson was one of those imaginary friends that some children make up when they feel lonely.

'Poor Smidge,' said Mum. 'Seb and Sally are much older than him, after all. He hasn't got anybody to play with. That's why he makes up stories about this Karlsson.'

'Yes, we really must buy him a dog,' said Dad. 'He's been asking for one for so long. And once he's got one, he'll forget about Karlsson.'

That was how Smidge came to get Bumble. He got a dog all of his own, on his eighth birthday.

And that was the very day Mum and Dad and Seb and Sally finally saw Karlsson. Yes, they actually saw him! And this is how it happened:

Smidge was having his birthday party in his room. He had invited round Kris and Jemima, who were in his class at school. And when Mum and Dad and Seb and Sally heard all the chat and laughter coming from Smidge's room, Mum said:

'Come on, let's go and have a look at them! They're so cute, aren't they?'

'Yes, let's,' said Dad.

And who should they see when they peeped into Smidge's room, Mum and Dad and Seb and Sally? Who should be sitting there at the birthday tea table with cream cake all over his face, stuffing himself fit to burst, but a fat little man who yelled:

'Heysan hopsan, my name's Karlsson on the Roof. I don't think you've had the pleasure of meeting me before, have you?'

Mum nearly fainted then. And Dad was extremely worried.

'Don't tell anybody about this,' he said, 'not anybody.'

'Why?' asked Seb.

And Dad explained why.

'Think what a fuss there'd be if people found out about Karlsson being here. He'd be on television, you know. We'd be tripping over television cables and cameras on the stairs, and every half hour we'd have a newspaper photographer at the door, asking to take pictures of Smidge and Karlsson. Poor Smidge. He'd be "The boy who found Karlsson on the Roof " . . . We'd never have a moment's peace as long as we lived.'

Mum and Seb and Sally could see that, so they all promised faithfully not to tell anyone about Karlsson.

Now it so happened that Smidge was going to his granny's in the country the next day, to stay for the summer holidays. He was looking forward to it, but he was worried about Karlsson. How would Karlsson keep himself busy in the meantime? What if he disappeared and never came back?

'Please, Karlsson, you are sure you'll still be living up there on the roof when I get back from Granny's, aren't you?' Smidge asked him.

'You never know,' said Karlsson. 'I'm going to my granny's too. She's much grannier than yours, and she thinks I'm the best grandson in the world. So you never can tell . . . she'd be daft to let the best grandson in the world go, wouldn't she?'

'Where does she live, your granny?' asked Smidge.

'In a house,' said Karlsson. 'Did you think she'd be running around all night without a roof over her head?'

That was all Smidge could find out. And the next day he went to his granny's. He took Bumble with him. It was fun being in the countryside, and Smidge was out playing all day. He didn't think about Karlsson all that much. But when the summer holidays were over and he came back to Stockholm, he asked about Karlsson the minute he got through the door.

'Mum, have you seen Karlsson at all?'

Mum shook her head.

'No, I haven't. I expect he's moved house.'

'Don't say that,' said Smidge. 'I want him still to be living up on our roof. He's got to come back.'

'But you've got Bumble, anyway,' Mum said, trying to console him. She thought it was a great relief to be rid of Karlsson.

Smidge patted Bumble.

'Yes, I know I have. And he's great. But he hasn't got a propeller and he can't fly, and there are more games you can play with Karlsson.'

Smidge ran into his room and opened the window.

'Karlsson, are you up there?' he shouted at the top of his voice. But there was no answer. The next day, Smidge went back to school. He wasn't in the infants any longer. When he got home, he sat in his room doing his homework. He kept the window open, so he would hear the droning motor sound that usually meant Karlsson was on his way. But the only droning he heard was from the cars passing by in the street, and an occasional aeroplane flying over the rooftops, not a Karlsson sort of drone.

'I suppose he must have moved house, after all,' said Smidge sadly to himself. 'I'm sure he won't ever come back.'

When he was lying in bed in the evenings, he thought about Karlsson, and sometimes he had a quiet little cry under the covers because Karlsson was gone. The days passed, with school and homework and no Karlsson.

One afternoon, Smidge was in his room sorting out his stamp collection. He already had lots of stamps in his album, but there were some others waiting to be put in. Smidge set to work, sticking them in place. Soon he had only one loose stamp left, his best one, which he had saved for last. It was a German stamp, with Red Riding Hood and the wolf on it, and Smidge really liked the picture. He put it on the table in front of him.

Just then he heard a buzz outside the window. A buzz that sounded like . . . yes, it certainly sounded like Karlsson! And it *was* Karlsson. He zoomed in through the open window and shouted:

'Heysan hopsan, Smidge.'

'Heysan hopsan, Karlsson!' shouted Smidge. He jumped to his feet, happy as can be, and watched Karlsson fly a couple of times round the ceiling light, before landing in front of him with a little thud. As soon as Karlsson had switched off his motor—which he did by turning a little winder on his tummy—Smidge tried to rush over and give him a hug, but Karlsson pushed him away with his podgy little hand and said:

'Easy now, take it easy! Is there anything to eat? Any meatballs or anything? Or perhaps a bit of cream cake?'

Smidge shook his head.

'No, Mum hasn't made any meatballs today. And cream cake is only for birthdays.'

Karlsson snorted.

'What sort of family do you call this? "Only for birthdays" . . . but what about when a dear old friend you haven't seen for months turns up? Might have expected that to spur your mum into action.'

'Yes, but we didn't know . . . ' began Smidge.

'Didn't know,' said Karlsson. 'You could have hoped! You could have hoped I'd come today, and that should've been enough to get your mum making meatballs with one hand and whipping cream with the other.'

'We only had sausage for lunch,' said Smidge, shamefaced. 'But if you'd like . . . '

'Boring old sausage, when a dear friend you haven't seen for months is coming?'

Karlsson gave another snort.

'I suppose if you want to be a regular visitor in this house, you have to learn to put up with anything . . . bring me some of that sausage,' he said.

Smidge dashed to the kitchen as fast as he could. Mum wasn't in; she'd gone to the doctor's, so he couldn't ask her. But he knew it would be all right to offer Karlsson some sausage. There were five leftover slices on a plate, so he took them in to Karlsson. And Karlsson pounced on them like a hawk. He stuffed his mouth full of sausage and looked very pleased.

'Well,' he said, 'as sausage goes, it doesn't taste too bad. Not like meatballs, of course, but you can't expect much of some people.'

Smidge realized who Karlsson meant when he said 'some people', so he quickly changed the subject.

'Did you have a good time at your granny's?' he asked.

'I had such a good time, I can't tell you,' said Karlsson. 'So I'm not going to tell you,' he said, and took another hungry bite of sausage.

'I had a good time, too,' said Smidge. He started telling Karlsson all the things he had done at granny's.

'She's so very, very nice, *my* granny,' said Smidge. 'And you wouldn't believe how glad she was to see me. She gave me the hardest hug she could.'

'Why?' asked Karlsson.

'Because she likes me, of course,' said Smidge.

Karlsson stopped chewing.

'And I suppose you think *my* granny doesn't like me all that much, eh? You don't believe she threw herself on me and hugged me until I went blue in the face, just because she liked me so much, do you, eh? But let me tell you, my granny's little fists are as hard as iron, and if she'd liked me just an ounce more, I wouldn't have been sitting here now, because she'd have crushed me to death.'

'Really?' said Smidge. 'She must be a champion at hugging, your granny.'

His granny hadn't hugged him that hard, but there was no doubt that she liked him, and was always nice to him, as he explained to Karlsson.

'Though she is the world's worst nagger,' said Smidge after he'd thought for a bit. 'She nags on about changing my socks and not fighting with Lars Jansson and stuff like that.'

Karlsson discarded the plate, which was now empty.

'And I suppose you think my granny isn't much good at nagging, eh? You don't believe she set the alarm clock to ring its head off at five every morning, just so she'd have enough time to nag me about changing my socks and not fighting Lars Janson?'

'Do you know Lars Jansson?' asked Smidge in surprise.

'No, thank goodness,' said Karlsson.

'So why did your granny say . . . ' asked Smidge. 'Because she's the world's naggiest nagger,' said Karlsson. 'Maybe you can see that now. You actually know Lars Jansson, so how can you have the cheek to claim your granny's the naggiest nagger? No, give me my granny any day. She can spend a whole day nagging me not to fight Lars Jansson, even though I've never seen the boy and hope I'll never have to, either.'

Smidge thought about this. It certainly was strange . . . he hadn't liked it at all when Granny nagged him, but all of a sudden he felt he had to try to outdo Karlsson by making Granny a worse nagger than she was.

'As soon as I got my feet the tiniest bit wet, she started nagging me to change my socks,' he told Karlsson.

Karlsson nodded.

'And I suppose you think my granny didn't want me to change my socks, eh? You don't believe she came rushing after me through the village when I was out and happened to step in a puddle, and nagged on and on: "Change your socks, Karlsson dear, change your socks" . . . you don't believe me, do you?'

Smidge squirmed. 'Well, maybe . . .'

Karlsson pushed Smidge down onto a chair and planted himself in front of him, hands on hips.

'Nope, you don't believe me. But just you listen and I'll tell you what happened. I was out, and stepped in a puddle, see? I was having a great time. But in the middle of it all, up sprints Granny, hollering so loud the whole village can hear: "Change your socks, Karlsson dear, change your socks".'

'And what did you say?' asked Smidge.

' "Not likely," I said, "because I'm the world's

most disobedient Karlsson",' declared Karlsson. 'So I ran away from Granny and climbed up a tree for a bit of peace and quiet.'

'I expect she felt let down,' said Smidge.

'I can tell you don't know my granny,' said Karlsson. 'She followed me.'

'Up the tree?' asked Smidge in astonishment.

Karlsson nodded.

'But of course, you don't believe my granny can climb trees, do you? Oh yes, if there's nagging to be done, she can clamber up to any height. "Change your socks, Karlsson dear, change your socks," she said, and crawled out along the branch I was sitting on.'

'So what did you do next?' asked Smidge.

'Well, what could I do?' said Karlsson. 'I changed my socks, she wouldn't settle for anything less. High up in a tree, on a shaky little branch, risking my life, I sat there and changed my socks.'

'Hah, I know you're lying now,' said Smidge. 'You couldn't possibly have had any socks up in the tree to change into.'

'How stupid can you get?' said Karlsson. 'What do you mean, I didn't have any socks to change into?'

He hauled up his trouser legs and pointed to his little fat legs in their saggy, stripy socks.

'What are these, then?' he said. 'Socks, wouldn't you say? Two of them, if I'm not mistaken. So didn't I sit there on my branch and change them, put the left sock on my right foot and the right sock on my left foot, didn't I, eh? Just to keep my old granny happy?'

'Yes, but that couldn't have helped get your feet any drier,' said Smidge.

'Have I ever claimed it did?' asked Karlsson. 'Have I?'

'But then . . .' stammered Smidge, 'then there was no point you changing your socks!'

Karlsson nodded.

'So you see now who's actually got the world's naggiest nagger for a granny? Your granny nags because she has to, with a grandson as stubborn as you. But mine's the world's naggiest, because she nags me for no reason at all; have you finally got that into your poor skull, eh?'

Then Karlsson let out a guffaw of laughter and gave Smidge a little shove.

'Heysan hopsan, Smidge,' he said. 'Now let's

both forget our grannies; I think it's time to have some fun.'

'Heysan hopsan, Karlsson. I think so too.'

'Have you got a new steam engine?' asked Karlsson. 'Remember what fun we had blowing up the last one? Have you got a new one, so we can do it again?'

But Smidge hadn't got a new steam engine, and Karlsson didn't look at all happy about that. Just then, luckily, he caught sight of the vacuum cleaner Mum had accidentally left in Smidge's room after she'd finished vacuuming in there earlier. With a little shriek of delight, Karlsson rushed over and turned it on.

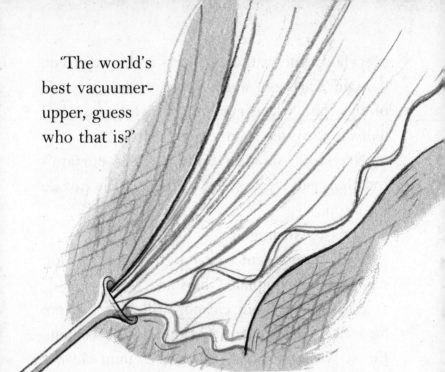

'The world's best vacuumer-upper, guess who that is?'

And he started vacuuming for all he was worth.

'If I can't have things all nice and tidy around me, then you can count me out,' he said. 'This filthy place needs a good going over. What luck for you and your family that the world's best vacuumer-upper happens to be here.'

Smidge knew Mum had given the whole room a very thorough vacuuming, and he said so, but Karlsson gave a scornful laugh.

'Women can't handle this sort of equipment;

everybody knows that. No, this is the way to do it,' said Karlsson, and started vacuuming one of the thin, white curtains, which got sucked halfway into the cleaner with a little hiss.

'No, stop,' shouted Smidge. 'The curtain's too thin, can't you see it's stuck in the nozzle . . . Stop!'

Karlsson shrugged.

'Well, if you want to live in filth and squalor, who am I to complain?' he said.

With the vacuum cleaner still switched on, he started pulling and tugging at the curtain. But it was stuck fast, and the vacuum cleaner wouldn't let go.

'None of your tricks,' said Karlsson to the cleaner. 'Because what you've got here is Karlsson on the Roof, the world's best tug-of-war champion.'

He gave a mighty tug and out came the curtain.

But it was rather black, and a bit tattered as well.

'Oh no, look at the curtain,' said Smidge unhappily. 'Look, it's all black!'

'What did I say? But you, you little pig, you tell me a curtain like this doesn't need vacuuming,' said Karlsson.

He patted Smidge on the head.

'But don't get upset, you might turn out all right in the end, in spite of your grubby habits. Come to think of it, I'd better vacuum you a bit . . . or has your mum already done you?'

'No, she definitely hasn't,' said Smidge.

Karlsson came hurrying over, brandishing the nozzle.

'There, that's women for you,' he said. 'Vacuum the whole room and forget the dirtiest bit! Come on, we'll start with your ears!'

Smidge had never been vacuumed before, but now he found out how it felt, and it tickled so much that he hooted with laughter.

Karlsson made a proper job of it. He vacuumed Smidge's ears and hair and neck and armpits and back and tummy, and right down to his feet.

'This is what they call a good autumn cleaning,' said Karlsson.

'If you knew how much it tickles,' said Smidge.

'Yes, you really ought to pay extra for that,' said Karlsson.

Then Smidge wanted to give Karlsson a good autumn cleaning.

'It's my turn now. Come on, I'll vacuum your ears!'

'No need,' said Karlsson, 'because I washed them last September. There are much more urgent things round here.'

He looked about the room and noticed Smidge's stamp lying on the table.

'Horrid little bits of litter everywhere, messing the place up,' he said. And before Smidge could stop him, he had sucked Red Riding Hood into the vacuum cleaner.

Smidge was appalled.

'My stamp,' he shouted. 'Now you've sucked up Red Riding Hood and I'll never forgive you.'

Karlsson turned off the vacuum cleaner and folded his arms.

'Pardon *me*,' he said. 'Pardon me for being a kind and helpful and hygienic little Karlsson just trying to do his best here in life; pardon me for that!'

He sounded as if he might be about to cry.

'It's no use,' he said, his voice quavering. 'I never get any thanks . . . just more and more tellings off!'

'Oh,' said Smidge, 'please don't be sad, but

you see Red Riding Hood . . . '

'What's this old red riding hood you're so worked up about?' asked Karlsson, who by now had decided not to cry.

'She's on the stamp,' said Smidge. 'My best stamp.' Karlsson just stood there, pondering. Then his eyes began to gleam and he smiled a knowing smile.

'The world's best pretend game player, guess who that is? And guess what we're going to play? Red Riding Hood and the wolf! We'll pretend the vacuum cleaner's the wolf and I'm the hunter who comes and slits open the wolf's belly, and hey presto, out comes Red Riding Hood!'

He looked round eagerly.

'Have you got an axe anywhere? Vacuum cleaners like this are as hard as iron.'

Smidge hadn't got an axe, and he was glad he hadn't.

'But you can always open the vacuum cleaner and pretend you're slitting open the wolf's belly.'

'If you want to cheat, yes,' said Karlsson. 'That's not what I *usually* do when I slit wolves open, but since there's no stuff in this useless house, I suppose we'll just have to pretend!'

He threw himself tummy first on top of the vacuum cleaner and bit the handle.

'You stupid thing!' he shouted. 'Why did you suck up Red Riding Hood?'

Smidge thought Karlsson was very childish, playing such babyish games, but it was still fun to watch.

'Easy now, take it easy, Little Red Riding Hood,' shouted Karlsson. 'Get your hat and galoshes on, because you're coming out right now!'

So Karlsson opened the vacuum cleaner, and emptied everything inside it onto the rug. It made a horrible big, grey pile.

'Oh dear, you should have emptied it into a paper bag,' said Smidge.

'Paper bag . . . is that what it says in the fairytale, eh?' said Karlsson. 'Does it say the hunter slit open the wolf's belly and emptied Red Riding Hood into a paper bag, eh?'

'Well, no,' said Smidge, 'of course not . . . '

'Right, so keep quiet then,' said Karlsson. 'Try not to invent bits that aren't in it, or you can count me out!'

Then he had to stop, because a gust of wind blew in through the window and lots of dust flew up his nose. It made him sneeze. He sneezed right into the pile of dust and fluff. That blew a scrap of paper across the floor to land at Smidge's feet.

'Look, there's Red Riding Hood,' cried Smidge, quickly rescuing the little, fluff-covered stamp.

Karlsson looked pleased with himself.

'That's what I do,' he said. 'I find lost things with one big sneeze. So maybe now you'll stop kicking up such a fuss about Red Riding Hood!'

Smidge dusted off his stamp and felt pretty happy.

Then Karlsson sneezed again, and a cloud of dust rose from the floor.

'The world's best sneezer, guess who that is,' said Karlsson. 'I'm going to sneeze all the dust back into its proper place, you wait and see!'

Smidge wasn't listening. All he wanted was to get his stamp stuck in the album.

But Karlsson stood there in a cloud of dust, sneezing. He sneezed and sneezed, and by the time he'd finished sneezing, he'd sneezed away most of the pile of dust and fluff.

'There, I told you we didn't need a paper

bag,' said Karlsson. 'And now all the dust's back where you usually keep it. Everything in its place, that's what I like. If I can't have things all nice and tidy around me, then you can count me out!'

But Smidge was concentrating on his stamp. There, he'd stuck it in now, and it looked great!

'Have I got to vacuum your ears again?' said Karlsson. 'You're not listening, are you?'

'What did you say?' asked Smidge.

'What I said was that it can't be right that I'm the only one toiling away here and getting blisters on my hands. I've been cleaning and cleaning for you, so now it's not asking too much for you to come up and do some cleaning for me.'

Smidge tossed aside his stamp album. Go up on the roof with Karlsson? There was nothing he'd rather do! He'd only been up to Karlsson's little house on the roof once before. That time, his mum had created a huge scene and sent the fire brigade up to bring him down.

Smidge thought about it. That was ages ago, and he was much bigger now, the sort of age when you can climb about on any roof at all. But did Mum realize this, that's what he wanted to know. She wasn't in, of course, so he couldn't ask her. Perhaps it would be just as well not to ask.

'Are you coming, then?' asked Karlsson.

Smidge thought it over again.

'But what if you drop me when we're flying?' he said anxiously.

Karlsson didn't seem worried.

'Oh well,' he said, 'there are plenty of children. One kid more or less, that's a mere trifle.'

This made Smidge really cross.

'I'm not a mere trifle, and if I fall . . . '

'Easy now, take it easy,' said Karlsson, patting him on the head. 'You won't fall. I shall hold on to you as hard as Granny did. Because even though you're just a grubby little boy, I sort of like you, all the same. Especially now you've had your autumn cleaning and all that.'

He patted Smidge again.

'Yes, it's funny, but I like you all the same, silly little boy that you are. Just wait till we get up to the roof: I'll give you a hug hard enough to make your face turn blue, just like Granny did.'

He turned the winder on his tummy, his motor started whirring, and Karlsson took a firm grip on Smidge. Then they flew out of the window and up into the blue sky. The tattered curtain waved gently, as if it was trying to say goodbye.

At Home
with Karlsson

Little houses up on rooftops can look really inviting, especially those like Karlsson's. Karlsson's house has green shutters and a front porch with a little set of steps, excellent for sitting on. You can sit there in the evenings, looking at the stars, or in the daytime, drinking squash and eating biscuits, if you've got any biscuits, of course. At night you can sleep out there, if it happens to feel too hot indoors, and you can wake up there in the mornings and see the sun rise over the rooftops on the other side of town.

Yes, it really is an inviting house, and so

neatly squeezed in between a chimney stack and a fire wall that you can hardly see it. Unless you happen to be walking around up on the roof, of course, and find yourself just behind the chimney. But people don't often do that.

'Everything's so different up here,' said Smidge once he and Karlsson had landed on the front steps of Karlsson's house.

'Yes, thank goodness,' said Karlsson.

Smidge looked all round him.

'More roofs and so on,' he said.

'Miles and miles of roofs,' said Karlsson, 'just right for going round and jiggery-poking as much as you like.'

'Shall we jiggery-poke a bit now?' asked Smidge eagerly. He remembered how exciting it had been the last time he and Karlsson did some jiggery-pokery up on the roof together.

But Karlsson gave him a stern look.

'So you get out of the cleaning, I suppose? First I wear my fingers to the bone making your place all spick and span, and then you think you'll spend the rest of the day jiggery-poking. Is that what you'd reckoned on?'

Smidge hadn't reckoned on anything at all.

28

'I'll be glad to help with the cleaning, if it needs doing,' he said.

'I should think so, too,' said Karlsson.

He opened the door to his house, and Smidge stepped inside the home of the world's best Karlsson.

'Yes, by all means,' said Smidge, 'if it needs doing, let's . . . '

Then he just stood there saying nothing for a long time, his eyes almost popping out of his head.

'It needs doing,' he said in the end.

There was only one room in Karlsson's house. In that one room Karlsson had a carpentry bench to do carpentry on and eat at and put stuff on. And a settee with a lift-up seat, to sleep on and jump on and hide stuff in. And two chairs to sit on and put stuff on and climb on if he needed to put any stuff in his cupboard. Only he couldn't, because it was already so full of other stuff, stuff that couldn't be left on the floor or hung on the nails on the wall, because there was already other stuff there . . . quite a lot of it. Karlsson had an open fire with stuff in the fireplace and an iron grate to cook food on.

The mantelpiece was covered in stuff. But there was hardly any stuff at all hanging from the ceiling. Only a brace drill and a bag of nuts and a cap pistol and some big pincers and a pair of slippers and a carpentry plane and Karlsson's nightshirt and the dishcloth and the poker and a little rucksack and a bag of dried cherries, that was all.

Smidge just stood there in the doorway, taking it all in.

'There, that shut you up,' said Karlsson. 'There's plenty of stuff here, not like down at your place, where there's hardly any stuff at all.'

'Wow, there's stuff all right,' said Smidge. 'But I can see why you want to clean up.'

Karlsson threw himself onto the settee and settled back comfortably.

'You've got the wrong end of the stick there,' he said. 'I don't want to clean up. *You* want to clean up . . . after all my toiling down at your place, don't you?'

'Aren't you going to help even a little bit?' asked Smidge uneasily.

Karlsson snuggled into his pillow and grunted, the way you do when you feel really cosy.

'Yes, of course I'll help,' he said, when he had finished grunting.

'I'm glad about that,' said Smidge. 'I was afraid you were going to . . .'

'Yes, of course I'll help,' said Karlsson. 'I'll serenade you the whole time, to cheer you up. Ho ho, it'll be easy peasy.'

Smidge wasn't so sure. He hadn't had to do very much cleaning in his life. He was used to tidying away his toys, of course: Mum only had to tell him three or four or five times, and he just did it, even though he thought it was a bother and not really worth the effort. But cleaning up for Karlsson was quite a different matter.

'Where shall I start?' Smidge asked.

'Dozy boy, you start with the nutshells of course,' said Karlsson. 'Obviously there's no need for a serious cleaning session, because I sort of do it all as I go along, to stop the mess building up. A final polish is all we need.'

The nutshells were strewn about the floor among lots of other debris, like orange peel and cherry stones and sausage skin and balls of screwed up paper and used matches. The floor itself was not to be seen.

'Have you got a vacuum cleaner?' asked Smidge after a moment's thought.

That was plainly a question Karlsson didn't like. He looked crossly at Smidge.

'Some people are very lazy, I must say! I've got the world's best broom and the world's best dustpan, but that's not good enough for certain lazyboneses, oh no, they want vacuum cleaners, to get out of doing anything themselves.'

Karlsson gave a snort.

'I could have a thousand vacuum cleaners if I wanted. But I don't take things as easy as some people. I like exercise.'

'I think I do, too,' said Smidge apologetically, 'but . . . come to think of it, you haven't got any electricity for a vacuum cleaner, have you?'

He remembered now that Karlsson's house was very old-fashioned. There was no electricity or running water. Karlsson had an oil lamp for light in the evenings, and he got his water from the water butt just outside his house.

'You haven't got a rubbish chute either,' said Smidge, 'though you could really do with one.'

'So you think I haven't got a rubbish chute, eh?' said Karlsson. 'What do you know about it? You sweep up the rubbish, and I'll show you the world's best rubbish chute.'

Smidge sighed. He picked up the broom and set to work. Karlsson lay there watching with his hands clasped behind his head, looking very pleased with himself. He sang to Smidge, just as he'd promised:

'Lie down, lie down, young yeoman;
The sun moves always west;
The road one treads to labour
Will lead one home to rest,
And that will be the best.'

'Exactly so, quite right,' said Karlsson, adjusting his pillow to make himself even more comfortable. Then he sang it again, while Smidge went on sweeping. And in spite of Smidge being so busy, Karlsson suddenly said:

'While you're at it, could you make me a cup of coffee?'

'Me?' asked Smidge.

'Yes please,' said Karlsson. 'Though I don't want to put you to any extra bother. All you've

33

got to do is light the fire in the hearth and fetch some water and boil it up with the grounds from last time. I can drink the coffee for myself.'

Smidge dejectedly surveyed the floor, which was nowhere near having had its final polish yet.

'Can't you make the coffee while I do the sweeping?' he suggested.

Karlsson gave a heavy sigh.

'How does anybody get as bone idle as you?' he asked. 'Since you're at it anyway . . . can it be that hard to make a cup of coffee as well?'

'No, of course not,' said Smidge, 'but if you really want to know what I think . . . '

'No, I don't,' said Karlsson. 'Don't trouble yourself! Instead, try being a bit of a help to the person who's worn himself out for your sake, vacuumed your ears and I don't know what.'

Smidge put down the broom. He took a bucket and dashed out for some water. He grabbed some wood from the wood box and shoved it into the fireplace, and did his best to get a fire going, but it wouldn't catch light.

'I'm not used to this,' he said apologetically. 'Couldn't you . . . just light the fire, I mean?'

'Don't try that with me,' said Karlsson. 'If

I was up and about, it would be different, and I'd be able to show you what to do, but since I happen to be having a lie down, you can't expect me to do everything for you.'

Smidge could see that was fair enough. He tried again, and this time the fire started to crackle and sing.

'It's alight,' said Smidge with satisfaction.

'There, see! It just needed a bit more effort,' said Karlsson. 'Now put the coffee on and lay a nice little tray and get out some buns; you can finish sweeping while it comes to the boil.'

'And what about the coffee . . . are you sure you can drink that for yourself?' asked Smidge. He could really be quite sarcastic sometimes.

'Oh yes, I'll drink the coffee myself,' said Karlsson. 'But you can have a drop too, because I'm incredibly generous to my guests, you know.'

And once Smidge had finished his sweeping, and shovelled all the nutshells and cherry stones and crumpled paper into Karlsson's big rubbish bucket, he and Karlsson sat on the edge of Karlsson's bed and had coffee. They ate lots of buns, too. And Smidge sat thinking how much he liked it at Karlsson's, even though doing his final polish for him was hard work.

'So where's that rubbish chute of yours?' Smidge asked once he'd finished his last bite of bun.

'I'll show you,' said Karlsson. 'Bring the rubbish bucket and come with me!'

He led the way out to the front porch.

'There,' he said, pointing down towards the gutter.

'How . . . do you mean?' said Smidge.

'Go down there,' said Karlsson.

'That's the world's best rubbish chute you've got there.'

'You mean empty the rubbish into the street?' said Smidge. 'I don't think you can do that sort of thing.'

Karlsson snatched the rubbish bucket. 'That's what *you* think. Come and see!'

Clutching the bucket, he dashed off down the roof. Smidge was scared: what if Karlsson couldn't stop when he reached the gutter?

'Slow down!' screamed Smidge. 'Put your brakes on!'

And Karlsson did put his brakes on. But not until he was right at the edge of the roof.

'What are you waiting for?' called Karlsson.

'Come here!'

Smidge sat down on his backside and shuffled gingerly down to the gutter.

'The world's best rubbish chute . . . a twenty metre drop,' said Karlsson, and swiftly tipped the bucket upside down. A torrent of cherry stones, nutshells, and balls of paper went cascading down the world's best rubbish chute, straight onto the head of an elegant gentleman who was on the pavement, smoking a cigar.

'Oh no!' said Smidge. 'Oh no, look, it went all over him!'

Karlsson gave a shrug.

'Who asked him to walk right under my rubbish chute, eh? Right in the middle of my autumn cleaning!'

Smidge looked worried.

'Yes, but now I bet he's got nutshells inside his shirt and cherry stones in his hair, and that isn't very nice.'

'It's a mere trifle,' said Karlsson. 'If all you've got to worry about in life is a couple of nutshells down your shirt, you should be happy.'

But the gentleman with the cigar didn't seem very happy. They could see him shaking himself, and then they heard him shouting for the police.

'What a fuss some people make about little things,' said Karlsson. 'He should be grateful instead.

Because if the cherry stones take root in his hair, he might get a nice little cherry tree growing there, and then he'll be able to go around picking cherries and spitting out the stones all day long.'

There was no sign of the police in the street below. The man with the cigar had to take his nutshells and cherry stones home with him.

Karlsson and Smidge climbed back up the

roof to Karlsson's house.

'Come to think of it, I quite fancy spitting out some cherry stones, too,' said Karlsson. 'While you're at it, can you bring me the bag of cherries hanging from the ceiling in there?'

'Do you think I'll be able to reach?' asked Smidge.

'Climb on my carpentry bench,' said Karlsson.

So that was what Smidge did, and then Karlsson and Smidge sat on the front steps eating dried cherries and spitting the stones in all directions. They went rolling down the roof with a series of little rattles. It sounded so funny.

The daylight was starting to fade. A soft, warm, autumn twilight settled over all the roofs and houses. Smidge shifted a bit closer to Karlsson. He did like sitting there on the front steps, spitting out cherry stones as it grew darker and darker. The buildings suddenly looked different, dark and mysterious and, in the end, totally black. It was as if someone had cut them out of black paper with big scissors and stuck on squares of shiny yellow paper for the windows. More and more gleaming squares stood out against the blackness, as people switched on the lights in their houses. Smidge tried counting them: to start with there were only three, then ten, and then there were lots and lots. Inside, behind the windows, you could see people moving about, doing things, and it made you wonder what they were up to and who they were and why they lived just there, not anywhere else.

Well, Smidge wondered. Karlsson didn't.

'They have to live somewhere, poor souls,' said Karlsson. 'Not everybody can have a house on the roof. Not everybody can be the world's best Karlsson.'

Karlsson Tirritates
a Creepy Crawley

While Smidge was up at Karlsson's, Mum had been at the doctor's. It took longer than she expected, and by the time she finally got home, Smidge was sitting quietly in his room, looking at his stamps.

'Hello, Smidge,' said Mum. 'Busy with your stamps as usual?'

'Yes,' said Smidge. After all, it was true. He didn't say that he had been up on the roof not long before. He knew Mum was clever and understood almost everything, but he wasn't absolutely sure she would understand about climbing roofs. Smidge decided not to say anything about Karlsson. Not for now. Not until the whole family had gathered. It would be a big surprise to spring on them at the dinner table. Actually, Mum wasn't looking very happy. She had a frown line between her eyes that wasn't usually there. Smidge wondered why.

Then the rest of the family came home, and it was dinnertime, and they all sat round the table together, Mum and Dad and Seb and Sally and Smidge. They had stuffed cabbage leaves, and as usual, Smidge just poked the cabbage apart and left it. He didn't like cabbage. He only liked the bit inside. Lying at his feet under the table was Bumble, and he would eat absolutely anything. Smidge folded the cabbage leaves into a soggy little parcel and passed them down to Bumble.

'Mum, tell him he's not to do that,' said Sally. 'Bumble's going to get unbearable . . . just like Smidge.'

'Mm, yes,' said Mum. 'Mm, yes!' But she didn't seem to be listening.

'*I* had to eat up everything when I was little, you know,' said Sally.

Smidge stuck out his tongue at her.

'Oh did you? Well, it doesn't seem to have

done *you* much good.'

That made tears well up in Mum's eyes.

'Don't squabble, please,' she said. 'I can't bear to hear you.'

And then at last she told them why she wasn't happy.

'The doctor said I was anaemic. Totally exhausted, he said. I've got to go away for a rest . . . though goodness knows how.'

There was complete silence round the table. No one said a word for a long time. What awful news! Mum was ill, and they all felt really sad about it. And she'd got to go away, as well, which Smidge thought was even worse.

'I want you to be standing in the kitchen every day when I get home from school, in your apron, baking buns,' said Smidge.

'All you ever think about is yourself,' said Seb sternly.

Smidge hugged Mum tightly.

'Well, there won't be any buns, otherwise,' he said. But Mum wasn't listening again. She was saying something to Dad.

'We'll have to try to get a home help, but goodness knows how.'

Mum and Dad both looked upset. It was nothing like as nice at the dinner table as usual. Smidge realized something had to be done to cheer everyone up a bit, and who better to do it than him?

'Guess what, though? Something great's happened,' he said. 'Guess who's come back?'

'Who? Oh dear, not Karlsson?' said Mum. 'Don't tell me we've got him to worry about now, as well!'

Smidge gave her a reproachful look.

'I think it's fun having Karlsson around, not a worry.'

Seb laughed.

'Well, we're in for a wild time here. No Mum, just Karlsson and a home help running riot about the place.'

'Don't scare the life out of me,' said Mum. 'What if the home help sees Karlsson, what will happen then?'

Dad looked at Smidge severely.

'Nothing will "happen" at all. The home help mustn't see Karlsson or hear a word about him. Promise, Smidge?'

'Karlsson flies wherever he likes,' said Smidge.

'But I promise not to say anything about him.'

'Not to a soul,' said Dad. 'Don't forget what we agreed.'

'No, not to a *soul*,' said Smidge. 'Only to Miss at school.'

Dad shook his head.

'Most certainly not to your teacher! Not on any account!'

'Huh,' said Smidge. 'Well then, I definitely shan't say anything about the home help, either. Because a home help is much worse than Karlsson, that's for sure.'

Mum sighed.

'We don't even know that we'll be able to get a home help,' she said.

But she put an advert in the newspaper the very next day. Only one person answered. Her name was Miss Crawley, and she arrived a few hours later for an interview for the job. Smidge happened to have earache just then, and wanted to be as close to Mum as possible, preferably sitting on her lap, though he was really too big for that.

'But when you've got earache, you have to,' said Smidge, climbing onto Mum's lap.

Then there was a ring at the door. It was

Miss Crawley. Smidge wasn't allowed to stay on Mum's lap. But the whole time Miss Crawley was there, he hung about beside Mum's chair, pressing his poorly ear against her arm and moaning a bit whenever he felt a twinge of pain.

Smidge had hoped Miss Crawley would be young, pretty, and kind, a bit like his teacher at school. But she was just the opposite: a stern, elderly lady who seemed to have very firm opinions. She was tall and sturdily built, had several chins and, what's more, the sort of 'angry eyes' Smidge was so afraid of. He immediately knew he didn't like her. And Bumble must have felt the same way, because he barked for all he was worth.

'Oh, there's a dog,' said Miss Crawley.

Mum looked worried.

'Don't you like dogs, Miss Crawley?' she asked.

'I do if they're well trained.'

'I don't know that I'd call Bumble well trained, exactly,' said Mum, a bit embarrassed.

Miss Crawley nodded energetically.

'But he will be, if I decide to take this job.

46

I've dealt with dogs before.'

Smidge hoped fervently that she wouldn't decide to. Then he felt a twinge in his ear, and couldn't help giving a little moan.

'Well well, dogs that growl and kids that howl,' said Miss Crawley with a hint of a smile. It was meant to be a joke, but Smidge didn't think it was a very funny one, and he said quietly, as if to himself:

'And my shoes squeak, too.'

Mum heard him. She blushed and said quickly: 'I hope you like children, Miss Crawley. I expect you do, don't you?'

'Yes, if they're well trained,' said Miss Crawley, fixing Smidge with a stare.

Mum had that embarrassed look again.

'I don't know that I'd call Smidge well trained, exactly,' she mumbled.

'But he will be,' said Miss Crawley. 'Just you wait. I've dealt with children before.'

Smidge was scared now. He felt so sorry for the children Miss Crawley had dealt with before. Now he was going to be one of those children himself—no wonder he looked terrified.

Mum seemed a bit doubtful, too. She stroked

Smidge's hair and said:

'With this one, kindness is what works best.'

'But it doesn't always help, I've noticed,' said Miss Crawley. 'Children need a firm hand sometimes.'

Then Miss Crawley announced how much she would like to be paid and that she was to be called 'housekeeper' rather than 'home help', and everything was decided.

Then Dad arrived home from the office, and Mum introduced their visitor:

'Our housekeeper, Miss Crawley!'

'Our creepy-crawly,' said Smidge. Then he shot out of the room, as fast as he could. Bumble ran after him, barking furiously.

And the next day, Mum went off to Granny's. Everybody cried when she went, Smidge most of all.

'I don't want to be left alone with Creepy Crawley,' he sobbed.

Because that was how it was going to be, he knew it. Seb and Sally were at school until late afternoon, weren't they, and Dad didn't get back from work until five o'clock. For hours and hours of every day, Smidge would be left to struggle with Creepy Crawley all by himself. That was why he was crying.

Mum gave him a kiss.

'Now try to be a good boy . . . for me! And whatever you do, don't call her Creepy Crawley!'

The misery started the very next day, when Smidge got home from school. There was no Mum ready and waiting in the kitchen with hot chocolate and buns, just Miss Crawley, and she didn't seem at all pleased to see him.

'Snacks between meals spoil your appetite,' she said. 'There won't be any buns here.'

But she had made buns, all the same. There was a whole plateful of them, cooling by the open window.

'Yes, but . . . ' said Smidge.

'No buts,' said Miss Crawley. 'And incidentally, I don't want any children in the kitchen. Go to your room and do your homework, hang up your coat and wash your hands. Come on, quick march!'

Smidge went to his room, cross and hungry. Bumble was asleep in his basket, but he leapt up like a shot when Smidge came in. At least someone was pleased to see him. Smidge put his arms round Bumble.

'Has she been nasty to you, too? Ooh, I can't stand her! "Hang up your coat and wash your hands" . . . shall I air out the wardrobes and wash my feet as well, eh? I *usually* hang up my coat without anybody having to tell me, so there!'

He threw his coat into Bumble's basket, and Bumble at once lay down on it and started chewing one of the sleeves.

Smidge went over to the window and looked out. He stood there thinking how sorry for himself he felt and how much he was missing Mum. Then he suddenly saw something that cheered him up. Above the roof of the house opposite, Karlsson was practising his flying stunts. He was zooming to and fro between the chimneypots, and every so often he would turn a somersault in mid-air.

Smidge waved to him eagerly, and Karlsson came whizzing over at such a speed that Smidge had to jump aside to avoid a head-on collision as Karlsson zoomed in through the window.

'Heysan hopsan, Smidge,' said Karlsson. 'I haven't done you any harm, have I? So why are you looking so sulky? Are you all right?'

'No, I'm not. Not in the slightest,' said Smidge. And he told Karlsson the whole sorry tale. That Mum had gone away and they'd got a creepy-crawly instead, who nagged you and was horrible, and so mean she wouldn't even let you have a bun when you got home from school, even though there was a whole plate of them, freshly-baked, on the window ledge.

Karlsson's eyes began to sparkle.

'You're in luck,' he said. 'The world's best creepy-crawly tamer, guess who that is?'

Smidge knew straight away that it must be Karlsson. But he couldn't see how Karlsson could do anything about Miss Crawley.

'I'll start by tirritating her,' said Karlsson.

' "Irritating" you mean,' said Smidge.

Karlsson didn't like stupid comments like that.

'If I'd meant "irritating", I'd have said so. "Tirritating" is the same sort of thing, but more fiendish, you can hear that from how the word sounds.'

Smidge tried it out and had to agree Karlsson was right. 'Tirritate' sounded more fiendish.

'I think I'll start with a spot of bun tirritation,' said Karlsson. 'And you can help.'

'How?' asked Smidge.

'Pop into the kitchen and keep Creepy Crawley talking.'

'Yes, but . . . ' said Smidge.

'No buts,' said Karlsson. 'Keep her talking, so she has to take her eyes off the plate of buns for a minute.'

Karlsson chuckled. Then he turned his winder and his motor started to whirr. Chuckling merrily, he lined himself up and flew off through the window.

And Smidge headed boldly for the kitchen. Now he had the world's best creepy-crawly tamer to help him, he wasn't scared any longer.

Miss Crawley was even less pleased to see him this time. She was busy making herself some coffee, and Smidge could see she was about to treat herself to a coffee break with fresh buns. Apparently it didn't do adults any harm to have snacks between meals.

Miss Crawley gave Smidge a sour look.

'What do you want?' she asked, and her voice was as sour as her face.

Smidge thought for a minute; it was important to have something to talk about. But what on earth could he say?

'Guess what I'm going to do when I'm as big as you, Miss Crawley,' he said in the end.

At that moment he heard a whirr outside the window, and it was a whirr he recognized. But he couldn't see Karlsson. The only thing he could see was a podgy little hand reaching over the window sill and taking one of the buns from the plate. Smidge gave a giggle. Miss Crawley hadn't noticed anything.

'So what *are* you going to do when you get big?' she asked impatiently. It wasn't as if she really wanted to know. She just wanted to get rid of Smidge as soon as possible.

'Guess,' said Smidge.

Then he saw the podgy little hand swish past once more, taking another bun from the plate. And Smidge giggled again. He tried not to, but he couldn't help it. There was so much giggle welling up inside him and simply bubbling out. Miss Crawley looked annoyed. She clearly thought he was the most tiresome boy in the whole world. And just when she was about to enjoy her coffee break, too!

'Guess what I'm going to do when I'm as big as you,' he said, and then he giggled again. Because he saw two little hands grabbing the rest of the buns from the plate.

'I haven't time to stand here listening to your daft ideas,' said Miss Crawley, 'and I don't care what you want to be when you get big. But as long as you're still small, you're to be polite and obedient and do your homework and get out of my kitchen.'

'Yes, of course I will,' said Smidge, giggling so much he had to prop himself up against the door. 'But when I'm as big as you, I'm going to go on a slimming diet, that's one thing for sure.'

Miss Crawley looked as if she was going to make a grab for him, but at that very moment there was a sound like a mooing cow from the window. That made her suddenly turn round, and then she saw the buns were gone.

Miss Crawley gave a howl.

'Oh lordy lordy, where are my buns?'

She dashed to the window. Perhaps she thought she would see a thief running away, his arms full of buns. But the Stevensons lived on the fourth floor, of course, and she must have realized there were no thieves with legs that long.

Miss Crawley, horrified at the loss of her buns, sank down on a chair.

'Could it be pigeons?' she muttered.

'It sounded more like a cow,' said Smidge. 'Maybe there's a cow out flying today, one that likes buns.'

'Don't be stupid,' said Miss Crawley.

Then Smidge heard Karlsson's whirr outside the window again, and to stop Miss Crawley noticing it he began to sing at the top of his voice:

'A cow with glittery wings
comes hovering down from the skies
a cow who really loves buns
and steals them whatever their size.'

Smidge used to make up rhymes with Mum sometimes, and he thought this one about the cow wasn't bad. But Miss Crawley didn't agree.

'That's quite enough of your nonsense,' she cried.

At that instant, there was a loud chinking sound from over by the window that made them both jump with fright. Then they saw what had made the sound. On the empty bun plate lay a small, five öre coin.

Smidge went off into another fit of giggles.

'What an amazing cow,' he said. 'She pays for her buns.'

Miss Crawley was red in the face with rage.

'What sort of stupid joke is this?' she roared,

rushing to the window. 'It must be somebody on the floor above, who thinks it's funny to steal buns and throw coins.'

'There isn't a floor above,' said Smidge. 'We live on the top floor. It's only the roof up there.'

Miss Crawley was beside herself.

'I don't understand it,' she screeched. 'I don't understand a thing.'

'No, so I've noticed,' said Smidge. 'But don't be sad about it, we can't all be clever.'

Then Smidge found himself on the receiving end of a clip round the ear.

'I'll teach you to be so cheeky,' yelled Miss Crawley.

'No, please don't,' said Smidge, 'because then Mum won't recognize me when she gets home.'

Smidge's eyes had glazed over. He was on the verge of tears. He had never had a clip round the ear before, and he didn't like it. He glared angrily at Miss Crawley. She took him by the arm and shoved him into his room.

'Now stay in there until you're sorry,' she said. 'I'm going to lock the door and take out the key. Then maybe you'll stop pestering me in the kitchen for a while.'

She looked at her watch.

'An hour should do, to make you into a good boy. I'll come and unlock the door at three. Until then you can think about what you're going to say when you apologize.'

And Miss Crawley went and left him. Smidge heard her turning the key. Now he was locked in and couldn't get out. It felt horrible. He was absolutely furious with Miss Crawley. But he also felt a bit guilty, because he hadn't really behaved very well either. Mum would be sure to think he had teased Creepy Crawley and been cheeky to her.

Mum, oh yes . . . for a while he wondered whether he might not have a little cry after all.

But then he heard a whirr, and in through the window flew Karlsson.

Karlsson's Invitation
to a Bun Feast

'**H**ow do you fancy a little snack between meals?' said Karlsson. 'Hot chocolate and buns on my front porch . . . the refreshments are on me!'

Smidge just looked at him. Oh, there was no one as wonderful as Karlsson; Smidge felt like hugging him. He tried to, as well, but Karlsson pushed him away.

'Easy now, take it easy! You're not at your granny's now. Well, are you coming?'

'Wow, yes!' answered Smidge. 'But actually, I'm locked in. I'm being kept prisoner in here.'

'That's what Creepy Crawley thinks,'

said Karlsson. 'And she can carry on thinking it for a while.'

His eyes started to gleam, and he did a whole series of delighted little hops in front of Smidge.

'Do you know what? We'll play that you're in a dungeon and having a ghastly time with a horrible creepy-crawly as your guard, and then along comes a terribly brave, strong, handsome, perfectly plump hero and rescues you.'

'What hero?' asked Smidge. Karlsson gave him a reproachful look.

'Try guessing, why don't you!'

'Oh, you mean you,' said Smidge. 'Then I think you ought to rescue me right away.'

Karlsson was happy to oblige.

'Because he's super quick, too, this hero,' Karlsson assured him. 'Quick as a hawk, oh yes, and brave and strong and handsome and perfectly plump, and he comes dashing in and saves you and is as brave as brave can be. Whoop, whoop, here he comes!'

Karlsson took a firm grip on Smidge and rose quickly and valiantly into the air. Bumble barked when he saw Smidge disappearing out of the window, but Smidge shouted:

'Easy now, take it easy! I'll be back soon.'

Up on Karlsson's front porch, ten buns were laid out in a row, looking very tempting.

'Honestly paid for, every single one,' said Karlsson. 'We'll divide them equally, seven for you and seven for me.'

'That won't work,' said Smidge. 'Seven and seven makes fourteen, and there are only ten buns.'

Karlsson hurriedly raked seven of the buns into a little pile.

'Well these are mine, at any rate,' he said, putting a podgy hand over the pile of buns. 'They teach you children such a daft way of counting at school these days. But I shouldn't have to suffer for it. We'll take seven each, like I said, and these are mine.'

Smidge nodded.

'I can't manage more than three, anyway. But where's the hot chocolate?'

'Down there with Creepy Crawley,' said Karlsson. 'And that's where we're going now, to fetch it.'

Smidge looked at him in alarm. He didn't

relish the thought of another meeting with Miss Crawley, and the possibility of more clips round the ear. Nor did he see how they could get at the cocoa tin. After all, it wouldn't be standing at the open window like the buns had been, but on a shelf by the stove, right in front of Miss Crawley's nose.

'How on earth will we do that?' asked Smidge.

Karlsson chuckled and looked pleased with himself.

'Well, I wouldn't expect a little ignoramus like you to be able to work it out! But the world's best jiggery-poker happens to have taken charge of things, so you can relax.'

'Yes, but how . . . ' began Smidge.

'Well,' said Karlsson, 'haven't you noticed that your block of flats has got balconies for beating carpets on?'

Smidge had, of course. Mum used to shake out their kitchen rugs on their balcony. It was very handy, just half a flight of stairs up from their kitchen door.

'Only ten steps from your door,' said Karlsson. 'Even a little dawdler like you should be able to toddle that distance fairly quickly.'

Smidge couldn't see what he meant.

'What am I supposed to be doing on the balcony?'

Karlsson sighed.

'Do I have to explain everything, you stupid little boy, you? Well, pin back your lugholes and I'll tell you my plan.'

'I'm listening,' said Smidge.

'Right then,' said Karlsson. 'Stupid little boy lands on the balcony courtesy of Karlsson Airlines, toddles down half a flight of stairs and rings long and hard on the doorbell, get it? Angry Creepy Crawley in the kitchen hears the bell and stomps off to open the door . . . so the kitchen's empty! Bold and perfectly plump hero flies in through the window and straight out again with the tin of cocoa in his hand. Stupid little boy rings again, just to be extra annoying, and runs back to the balcony. Angry Creepy Crawley opens the door and is angrier still when there's nobody standing out there with a bunch of red roses for her. She lets out a roar and slams the door. Stupid little boy stays giggling on the balcony until perfectly plump hero comes to fetch him for a bun feast on the roof. Heysan hopsan, Smidge, guess who's the world's best jiggery-poker . . . now let's get to work!'

And before Smidge could say a word, he was on his way from the roof to the carpet-beating balcony. Karlsson went into such a nose dive that the wind whistled round Smidge's ears and he had worse butterflies in his tummy than he'd had on the big dipper at Gröna Lund funfair. Then everything happened exactly as planned. Karlsson whirred off to the kitchen window while Smidge scuttled down and rang the doorbell long and hard. He soon heard footsteps inside, coming to the door. Then yes, you've got it, he giggled and dashed back to the balcony. A second later, the door opened down there and Miss Crawley stuck her head out. He could see her, if he peeped carefully through the glazed part of the balcony door. And it was obvious Karlsson had been right: angry Creepy Crawley was even more angry to find nobody outside the door. She muttered loudly to herself, and loitered in the doorway for a long while, as if expecting whoever had rung suddenly to appear before her eyes. But whoever had rung was stifling his giggles on the balcony, and he went on doing it until the perfectly plump hero came and fetched him for a bun feast on the hero's front porch.

It was the best bun feast Smidge had ever been to.

'Now everything feels much better,' he said as he sat on the step beside Karlsson, munching his bun and drinking his chocolate and looking out over the roofs and steeples of Stockholm as they glinted in the sunlight. The buns were delicious, and the chocolate was excellent too. He had made it himself over Karlsson's open fire. Karlsson had brought everything they needed, milk, cocoa, and sugar, from the kitchen below.

'And properly paid for every last bit, with a five öre coin I left on the kitchen table,' said Karlsson. 'If you're honest, then you're honest, and there's nothing to be done about it.'

'Where did you get all these coins from?' asked Smidge.

'From a wallet I found in the street the other day,' said Karlsson. 'Full of five öre pieces and other cash!' 'I feel sorry for whoever dropped the wallet,' said Smidge. 'I bet they were fed up.'

'Oh well,' said Karlsson, 'if you're a taxi

driver, I reckon you need to keep an eye on your things!'

'How do you know it was a taxi driver?' asked Smidge in surprise.

'I saw him drop the wallet, of course,' said Karlsson. 'And I could tell he was a taxi driver by the badge on his cap. I'm not that stupid, you know.'

Smidge gave Karlsson a reproving look. You really couldn't do that sort of thing with any lost property you found; he would *have* to tell Karlsson. But it needn't be now . . . another time would do! For now, he just wanted to sit here on the step, enjoying the sunshine and the buns and the chocolate and Karlsson.

Karlsson had already almost polished off his seven buns. Smidge couldn't eat that fast. He was finishing his second bun. The third one was on the step beside him.

'Oh, I feel better now,' said Smidge.

Karlsson leant forward and looked him straight in the eye. 'No, you don't. You don't feel well at all.'

He put his hand on Smidge's brow.

'Just as I thought! A clear case of bun fever.'

Smidge looked surprised. 'What's that . . . bun fever?'

'It's what you get from eating too many buns.'

'Then you must have it worse than me,' said Smidge.

'You might think so,' said Karlsson. 'But you see, I had bun fever when I was three, and you can only get it once, just like measles and whooping cough.'

Smidge didn't feel ill in the slightest, and he tried to tell Karlsson so. But Karlsson forced him to lie down on the porch and eagerly splashed his face with chocolate.

'So you don't faint,' explained Karlsson. Then he grabbed Smidge's last bun.

'No more buns for you, it would mean certain death! But how lucky for this poor little bun that I'm here, otherwise he'd have been left all by himself, here on the step,' said Karlsson, and gobbled up the bun.

'Now he isn't so lonely any more,' said Smidge. Karlsson patted his tummy contentedly.

'No, he's with his seven friends now, and he's happy!'

Smidge was happy, too. He lay there on the

porch, feeling just fine in spite of the bun fever. He was full up, and didn't mind Karlsson taking that last bun at all. Then he looked at his watch. It was a few minutes to three. Smidge started laughing.

'Miss Crawley will be coming along any minute now to let me out. Ooh, I wish I could see her face when she goes into my room and I'm not there.'

Karlsson patted him kindly on the shoulder.

'Tell Karlsson all your little wishes, and he'll arrange everything for you. Just pop in and get my binoculars for me. They're hanging on the fourteenth nail along from the settee, pretty high up. Climb on my carpentry bench.'

Smidge giggled.

'But I've got bun fever, you said. Doesn't that mean I have to lie still?'

Karlsson shook his head.

'Lie there giggling? Think that helps cure bun fever? No, it's just the opposite: the more you zip round the roofs and houses, the sooner you'll be restored to good health. Any medical book will tell you that.'

And since Smidge was quite keen to be rid of

his bun fever, he ran obediently into the house and climbed onto the carpentry bench and unhooked the binoculars that were hanging on the fourteenth nail along from the settee. Hanging from the same nail was a picture with a little red cockerel in one corner. Karlsson had painted it himself.

It came back to Smidge now that Karlsson was the world's best cockerel painter. What he had painted was a 'Portrait of a Very Small and Lonely Red Cockerel'—or so it said on the picture. And it was quite true that this cockerel was smaller, lonelier, and redder than any Smidge had seen in his life. But he hadn't time to look at it any longer, because it was almost three o'clock, and he was in such a hurry.

Karlsson was ready for take off when Smidge came back with the binoculars, and before Smidge could open his mouth, Karlsson was whirring off with him across the street, where they landed on the roof opposite. Then Smidge understood.

'Hey, what a great lookout point, if you've got some binoculars and want to look into my room!'

'Well, we have, and we do,' said Karlsson, putting the binoculars to his eyes. Then he let

Smidge borrow them, too. And he could see his room as clearly as if he was in it. There was Bumble, asleep in his basket; there was Smidge's bed; there was his desk with his homework; and there was the clock on the wall. It struck three. But there was no sign of Miss Crawley.

'Easy now, take it easy,' said Karlsson. 'I know she's coming, because I can feel shivers down my spine and I'm getting goose pimples.'

He snatched the binoculars from Smidge and raised them to his eyes.

'What did I tell you? The door's opening, and here she comes, as cute and cuddly as a cannibal chief.'

He gave a big chuckle.

'Hah, her eyes are really popping out of her head now! Where's Smidge? What if he's fallen out of the window?'

And that must have been what Miss Crawley thought, because she dashed over to the window looking scared stiff. Smidge felt really sorry for her. She leant out and looked down into the street, as if she expected to see Smidge there.

'Nope, he's not there. Bad luck, eh?'

Miss Crawley looked reassured. She retreated into the room.

'She's looking for you now,' said Karlsson. 'She's looking in the bed . . . and behind the desk . . . and under the bed, oh yes, she is . . . and wait, she's going into the wardrobe; she must think you're lying in a little heap in there, crying.'

Karlsson gave another big chuckle.

'It's time to start jiggery-poking her,' he said.

'How?' asked Smidge.

'Like this,' said Karlsson. And before Smidge could object, Karlsson whisked him across the street and set him down just inside the window.

'Heysan hopsan, Smidge, be nice to Creepy Crawley,' said Karlsson. And he flew off.

Smidge didn't think much of that sort of

jiggery-poking. But it was up to him to do his best. So he tiptoed very, very quietly across the room, sat down at his desk and opened his book of sums. He could hear Miss Crawley rummaging around in the wardrobe. Tense with excitement, he waited for her to come out.

And she did. The first thing she saw was Smidge. She shrank back against the wardrobe door. From there she stood staring at him in complete silence. Then she blinked a couple of times as if to check she was seeing properly.

'Where in the world were you hiding?' she asked in the end.

Smidge looked up innocently from his sums.

'I wasn't hiding. I've just been sitting here doing my adding up. I didn't realize you were playing hide and seek, Miss Crawley. But that's all right . . . you get in the wardrobe again, and I'll be happy to look for you.'

Miss Crawley didn't reply. She stood there for a while, her mind working hard.

'Surely I can't be falling ill?' she mumbled. 'So many odd things seem to happen in this house.'

Just then, Smidge heard someone cautiously

locking the door from the other side. Smidge giggled.

The world's best creepy-crawly tamer had obviously flown in through the kitchen window to teach Creepy Crawley how it felt being locked in.

Miss Crawley didn't notice. She just stood there saying nothing, and looking puzzled.

'Very strange! Oh well, you can go out and play now, while I get the dinner.'

'Thanks very much,' said Smidge. 'I haven't got to be locked in any longer, then?'

'No, you haven't,' said Miss Crawley, going over to the door. She grasped the handle and pressed it down, once, and then again. But the door wouldn't open. Then she threw her whole weight against it. That didn't help. The door stayed firmly shut.

Miss Crawley let out a yell.

'Who's locked the door?' she screeched.

'I think you did, Miss Crawley,' said Smidge.

Miss Crawley snorted.

'Nonsense! How can the door be locked from the outside, when I'm on the inside?'

'I don't know,' said Smidge.

'Could it have been Seb or Sally?' wondered Miss Crawley.

'No, they won't be home from school yet,' Smidge told her.

Then Miss Crawley sat down heavily on a chair.

'You know what I think,' she said. 'I think there's a ghost in this house.'

Smidge nodded. Oh, it would be great if Miss Crawley thought Karlsson was a ghost, because then she might leave. Surely she wouldn't want to stay in a house that was haunted?

'Are you afraid of ghosts, Miss Crawley?' Smidge asked.

'Not at all,' said Miss Crawley. 'I'm glad of them! Just think, *I* can be on television now, too! You know they have a series where people talk about being haunted, and what's happened to me in a single day here would be enough for ten of those programmes.'

Miss Crawley looked very pleased.

'That'll annoy my sister Frida, you may be sure. Frida's been on television, see, talking about all the ghosts she's seen and the ghost voices she's heard, and I don't know what. But

I shall be able to go one better now.'

'Have you heard any ghost voices then, Miss Crawley?'

'Yes, don't you remember the mooing outside the window just now, when the buns went missing? I shall try to imitate that on television, so people can hear what it sounded like.'

And Miss Crawley gave such a moo that Smidge jumped clean out of his seat.

'Something like that,' said Miss Crawley with satisfaction. But then an even louder mooing came from outside, and Miss Crawley turned terribly pale.

'It's answering me,' she whispered. 'The ghost's answering me. I shall say that on television. Lordy lordy, how jealous Frida will be!' And she told Smidge how Frida had boasted on television about all her ghostly encounters.

'If you believed *her*, you'd think our part of Stockholm was teeming with ghosts, most of them in our flat, but never in my room, always in Frida's. And you know what? One evening a ghostly hand appeared and wrote a warning to Frida on the wall! And my goodness, she needed one,' said Miss Crawley.

'What sort of warning?' asked Smidge.

Miss Crawley thought for a minute.

'What was it again? Oh yes, I know, it said: Beware! Your boundlessly short days should be spent with more gravity!' said Miss Crawley.

Smidge didn't look as if he understood a word of it, and nor did he. Miss Crawley had to explain.

'It was a warning to Frida to change her ways and start living a better life, without so much silly nonsense.'

'And did she?' asked Smidge.

Miss Crawley sniffed.

'I wouldn't say she did, not at all. She still shows off and thinks she's a TV star, even though she was only on there once. But I know somebody who's going to go one better than her, now.'

Miss Crawley rubbed her hands. She was so much looking forward to going one better than Frida that she didn't care about being locked in with Smidge. She sat there quite happily, comparing Frida's hauntings with her own, until Seb got home from school.

Then Smidge shouted:

'Open the door! I'm locked in with Creep . . . Miss Crawley!'

Seb opened the door, very surprised.

'Whoever locked the two of you in here?' he asked.

Miss Crawley just looked mysterious.

'You can find that out from the television in due course.'

Then she was in a hurry to get the dinner ready. She strode off to the kitchen.

A moment later there was a loud scream from the kitchen. Smidge ran to investigate.

Miss Crawley was sitting on a chair, even paler than before, pointing open-mouthed at the wall.

It wasn't only Frida who got warnings written by ghostly hands, oh no! Miss Crawley had got one too. It was scrawled on the wall in big letters you could read from metres away.

'BEWARE! YOUR SHAMELESSLY

EXPENSIVE BUNS SHOULD BE

FILLED WITH MORE CINNAMON!'

Karlsson on the Box

Dad came home for dinner with something else to worry about. 'I'm sorry, you lot, but it looks as though you'll have to cope on your own for a couple of days. The people at work want me to fly to London for some meetings. How do you think it'll go?'

'It'll go fine,' said Smidge. 'As long as you don't get in the way of the propeller.'

That made Dad laugh.

'Well, I really meant how are things going to work out for you three, here at home without Mum or me.'

Seb and Sally couldn't see any problem. They

would even quite enjoy having their parents out of the way for once, Sally said.

'Yes, but what about Smidge?' said Dad.

Sally ruffled Smidge's mop of fair hair.

'I'll be just like a mother to him,' she assured Dad. But he wasn't convinced, and nor was Smidge.

'You're always running about with boys whenever anybody needs you,' Smidge muttered.

Seb tried to console him.

'But you've always got me.'

'Yeah, at the football pitch,' grumbled Smidge.

Seb laughed.

'That only leaves Creepy Crawley. She doesn't run about with boys or kick footballs.'

'No, worse luck,' said Smidge.

He sat trying to work out exactly how much he loathed Miss Crawley. But then he realized something odd—he wasn't cross with her any more. Not a bit cross. Smidge was amazed. How had that happened? Did just being locked in with a person for two hours teach you to put up with them? It wasn't that he suddenly liked Miss Crawley—far from it—but she seemed to have become a bit more human. Poor thing, having to live with that Frida! Smidge knew all about what it felt like having problems with your brothers and sisters. But at least Sally didn't spend her time boasting about ghosts on television, like Frida.

'I don't want you three left on your own overnight,' said Dad. 'The best thing will be to ask Miss Crawley to stay while I'm away.'

'So I've got to put up with her at night as well as in the day, have I?' asked Smidge. But inside he felt it was a good idea to have someone looking after them, even if it was only a creepy-crawly.

And Miss Crawley was more than happy to come and stay with the children. When she and Smidge happened to be alone together, she explained why.

'It's at night most hauntings happen, you see. So now I'm going to gather up enough of them for a television programme that will make Frida fall off her chair when she sees me in it.'

This worried Smidge. What if, while Dad was away, Miss Crawley let loads of television people into the building and one of them happened to catch sight of Karlsson, although he wasn't a ghost at all but just good old

Karlsson? And that would be the end of the peace and quiet Mum and Dad were so keen to hang on to. Smidge realized he'd have to warn Karlsson and tell him to be careful.

He wasn't able to do it until the following evening. He was on his own in the flat. Dad had already left for London, Seb and Sally were both out, doing their own thing, and Miss Crawley had just popped home to see Frida in Frey Street to ask her if she'd seen any ghosts recently.

'I'll be back soon,' she told Smidge as she left. 'If any ghosts turn up, ask them to take a seat and wait for me, ha ha ha!'

Miss Crawley didn't often tell jokes, and hardly ever laughed. And on the rare occasions when she did, you were grateful it didn't happen more often. But this time, she got quite carried away. Smidge could hear her laugh fading away down the stairs. It was the sort of laugh that echoed round the walls.

Almost immediately, Karlsson came flying in at the window.

'Heysan hopsan, Smidge, what shall we do now?' he asked. 'Got any steam engines we can explode or creepy-crawlies we can tirritate?

Anything will do, but I must have some fun, or you can count me out!'

'We can watch television,' suggested Smidge.

And just imagine, Karlsson turned out not to have a clue about television! He'd never seen a TV set in his whole life. Smidge took him into the sitting room and pointed proudly at their posh new set with its big screen.

'Look!'

'What's that box for?' asked Karlsson.

'It's not a box, it's television,' explained Smidge.

'What do you keep in a box like that?' asked Karlsson. 'Buns, by any chance?'

Smidge laughed.

'Not on your life! Here, I'll show you what it does.'

He switched on the set, and suddenly there was a man on the screen, talking about what the weather would be like in the north of Sweden.

Karlsson's eyes grew wide with surprise.

'How did you get him into the box?'

Smidge laughed.

'How do you think? He crawled in there when he was a baby, of course.'

'What do you keep him for?' Karlsson wanted to know.

'Hah, can't you tell I'm joking?' said Smidge. 'Of course he didn't crawl in there when he was a baby and we don't *keep* him for anything. He's just *there*, see, telling us what the weather's going to be like tomorrow. He's one of those weathermen, OK?'

Karlsson gave a giggle.

'So you have a special man stuffed in a box to tell you what the weather's going to do tomorrow? Why not wait and see! Or ask me . . . there's going to be thunder and rain and hail and storms and an earthquake. Happy now?'

'The coast of Norrland will have storms and rain tomorrow,' said the weatherman on the television screen.

Karlsson laughed delightedly.

'There, what did I tell you? Storms and rain!'

He went right up to the set and pressed his nose up against the weatherman's nose.

'And an earthquake too, don't forget that! Poor people up in Norrland, what terrible weather they're going to have! But they ought to be glad they're getting any weather at all.

What if they found themselves left without any?'

He gave the man on the screen a kindly pat.

'What a dinky little man,' he said. 'Smaller than me. I like that.'

Then he knelt down and investigated the underside of the set.

'So where did he get in exactly?'

Smidge tried to explain that it was just a picture on the screen, not a living person, but then Karlsson almost lost his temper.

'Pull the other one, you dummy! He's moving, isn't he? And do you find dead people talking about the weather in northern Norrland, eh?'

Smidge didn't know much about how television worked, but he did his best to explain it all to Karlsson. And there was that warning he needed to give Karlsson, too.

'Miss Crawley wants to be on TV, too, you know,' he began, but that made Karlsson roar with laughter.

'Creepy Crawley in a little box like that! That great lump, she'd have to fold herself in quarters.'

Smidge sighed. Karlsson clearly hadn't understood a thing. Smidge had to explain all over again. It seemed hopeless, but in the end he did at least get Karlsson to understand the remarkable way a gadget like this worked. Miss Crawley didn't have to crawl into the set herself; she could be sitting comfortably miles away, but you would still be able to see her on the screen as large as life, Smidge told him.

'Creepy Crawley as large as life . . . ugh, how awful,' said Karlsson. 'You'd be much better off throwing out the box or swapping it for one with buns in.'

Just then, a pretty television announcer came on to the screen. She gave such a charming smile that Karlsson's eyes nearly popped out of his head.

'Although,' he said, 'they would have to be *particularly* scrumptious buns. Because I can see there's more to this box than you might think at first.'

The announcer lady carried on smiling at Karlsson, and Karlsson smiled back. He nudged Smidge in the side.

'Look at that little princess. She likes me . . . oh yes, because obviously she can see I'm a handsome, thoroughly clever, perfectly plump man in my prime.'

The announcer's face suddenly disappeared. Instead there were two serious, ugly gentlemen who just talked and talked. Karlsson didn't like it. He started twiddling all the buttons and controls he could find.

'No, don't do that,' said Smidge.

'Got to. How else can I find that little princess again?' said Karlsson.

He twiddled away madly, but the announcer didn't come back. All that happened was that the ugly gentlemen got even uglier. They sprouted short, squat legs and very high foreheads. Karlsson laughed at them. He also kept himself amused for a good long time by turning the set on and off.

'Those blokes come and go exactly as I want them to,' he said smugly.

The two gentlemen just kept on talking and talking whenever Karlsson gave them a chance.

'I, for my part, am of the opinion . . . ' said one of them.

'I don't care,' said Karlsson. 'Go home to bed.'

He switched off the set with a loud click and laughed delightedly.

'Just think how annoyed that bloke will be

that he didn't get to tell us what he for his part is of the opinion!'

But now Karlsson was tired of the television and wanted some other amusement.

'Where's Creepy Crawley? Bring her here so I can figurate her.'

'Figurate . . . how does that go?' asked Smidge anxiously.

'Well,' said Karlsson, 'there are three ways to tame creepy-crawlies. You can tirritate them or jiggery-poke them or figurate them. They're all the same thing really, but when you figurate there's more close tackling.'

Smidge grew even more anxious. What if Karlsson actually started tackling Miss Crawley? Then she'd see him, and that most definitely wasn't supposed to happen. Smidge would have to keep a close eye on him all the time Mum and Dad were away, however hard that would be. He'd have to try to scare Karlsson somehow, so Karlsson had the sense to keep out of Miss Crawley's way. Smidge thought about it, and then he said cunningly:

'Hey, Karlsson, wouldn't you like to be on television?'

Karlsson shook his head violently.

'In that box? Me? Not while I've got the health and strength to fight them off.'

But then a thought seemed to strike him.

'Although . . . if that little princess was going to be there!'

Smidge told Karlsson firmly that there was no hope of that. Oh no, if Karlsson was on TV, it would be with Creepy Crawley, without a doubt.

Karlsson gave a start.

'Me and Creepy Crawley in the same box . . . watch out, if there hasn't already been an earthquake in northern Norrland, there'll be one then. Make a note of that! Whatever gave you such a ridiculous idea?'

So then Smidge told him about the ghost programme Miss Crawley was planning to star in on television, to make Frida fall off her chair.

'Has Creepy Crawley seen a ghost then?' asked Karlsson.

'No, she hasn't *seen* one,' said Smidge. 'But she's heard one mooing outside the window. She thinks you're a ghost.'

Then Smidge explained how they all fitted

together, Frida and Creepy Crawley and Karlsson and television, but if he had thought that would scare Karlsson, he was wrong. Karlsson slapped his knees and roared with delight, and when he had finished roaring he slapped Smidge on the back.

'Look after Creepy Crawley! She's the best bit of furniture you've got in this flat. Just you look after her! Because now we can really start to have some fun.'

'How?' asked Smidge, uneasily.

'Whoop!' cried Karlsson. 'Frida's not the only one who's going to be falling off her chair, oh no! Hold on to your seats, all you creepy crawlies and TV blokes, and just see who comes zooming in!'

Smidge grew even more worried.

'Who *is* going to come zooming in?'

'Your neighbourhood ghost,' cried Karlsson. 'Whoop, whoop!'

At that point, Smidge gave up. He had warned Karlsson and tried to do what Mum and Dad wanted. Karlsson would just have to have his own way. Because he always did, when it came to the crunch. Karlsson could jiggery-poke and play ghost and figurate as much as he liked. Smidge wasn't going to try to stop him any longer. And once he'd decided that, he had the feeling it was going to be a lot of fun. He remembered another time Karlsson had been a ghost, and had scared away some burglars who were trying to steal Mum's housekeeping money and all the silver cutlery. Karlsson hadn't forgotten it, either.

'Do you remember what fun we had?' he said. 'By the way, where's the ghost outfit I had that time?'

Smidge had to admit that Mum had taken it. She'd been pretty angry about the sheet Karlsson had ruined. But then she had mended the holes and made the ghost outfit back into a sheet.

Karlsson gave a snort when Smidge told him.

'That sort of interference really gets on my nerves. Nobody ever leaves anything alone in this house.'

He sat down on a chair and sulked.

'If this is how it's going to be, you can count me out. You'll have to get your own ghosts, the lot of you.'

But then he dashed across to the linen cupboard and opened the door.

'Lucky there are plenty more sheets.'

He grabbed one of Mum's finest linen sheets, but Smidge came rushing to rescue it.

'Oh no, not that! Leave that one alone . . . there are some old, worn-out sheets here. They'll do.'

Karlsson didn't look impressed.

'Worn-out sheets! I thought the Neighbourhood Ghost would be all dressed up in his Sunday best. But all right, that's fine by me . . . I know this isn't one of the better houses . . . pass me the old rags!'

So Smidge rooted around for a pair of old sheets, and gave them to Karlsson.

'If you sew them together, they'll make a decent ghost outfit,' he said.

Karlsson stood grimly clutching the sheets.

'If *I* sew them together! If *you* sew them together, you mean. Come on, we'll fly up to my house, so Creepy Crawley doesn't come bursting in while you're busy stitching!'

Smidge spent the next hour sitting up at Karlsson's making a ghost outfit. At school he'd learnt running stitch, backstitch, and cross-stitch, but nobody had shown him how to sew together two worn-out sheets to make a ghost costume. He had to try to work it out for himself. He had a half-hearted try at getting Karlsson to help.

'You could at least do the cutting out,' said Smidge.

Karlsson shook his head.

'The only cutting out I'm likely to do is your mum, I'd like to cut her out of my life. Why did she have to go and take my ghost outfit, I'd like to know! It's only right and proper that you should have to make me a new one. Now get started and stop whinging!'

What was more, claimed Karlsson, he simply hadn't got time for any sewing, because he needed to paint a picture, double quick.

'That's what you have to do when inspiration comes, you know, and mine has just come. I heard a plop, and there it was!'

Smidge didn't know what inspiration was. But Karlsson explained that it was a sort of illness that struck down all picture painters and made them want to paint and paint instead of making ghost outfits.

So Smidge climbed onto the carpentry bench and sat cross-legged like a tailor, snipping and sewing while Karlsson made himself comfortable in the corner by the fireplace and got on with his picture. Outside it was pitch dark, but inside Karlsson's house it was light and cosy, the oil lamp was giving off a glow, and a fire was burning in the grate.

'I hope you've been paying attention in your sewing lessons,' said Karlsson, 'because I do want my ghost costume to look smart. I rather fancy a bit of blanket stitch round the neck, or maybe some feather stitching.'

Smidge didn't answer. He just kept sewing away, the fire crackled and Karlsson painted.

'What are you painting?' asked Smidge.

'I'll show you when it's finished,' said Karlsson.

Smidge finally managed to patch together a ghost outfit he thought might do. Karlsson tried it on and was very pleased with it. He flew a few circuits of the room to show it off.

Smidge gave a shiver. He thought Karlsson looked awfully spooky. Poor Miss Crawley:

ghosts were what she wanted, of course, but now she would be getting one that could scare the wits out of anybody.

'Creepy Crawley can send for those TV blokes now,' said Karlsson. 'Because the Neighbourhood Ghost is on his way, motorized, wild and wonderful, and *extremely* dangerous.'

Karlsson carried on flying round the room, chuckling smugly. He wasn't bothered about his painting any more. Smidge went over to see what Karlsson had painted.

'Portrait of my Rabbits', he had written at the bottom. But what Karlsson had painted was a small red creature that looked more like a fox.

'Isn't that a fox?' asked Smidge.

Karlsson came hovering down to land beside him. He put his head on one side and squinted at his picture.

'Yes, it's a fox all right. A fox painted by the world's best fox painter.'

'But,' objected Smidge, 'it says "Portrait of my Rabbits" . . . so where are the rabbits?'

'They're in the fox,' said Karlsson.

Karlsson's
Ingenious Bell

The next morning, Seb and Sally both woke up with a strange red rash on their bodies.

'Scarlet fever,' said Miss Crawley, once she had inspected them. The doctor she sent for said the same thing.

'Scarlet fever! Off to hospital for observation, the pair of you, right away!'

Then he pointed at Smidge.

'And this one's to be kept in quarantine until further notice.'

Smidge started crying when he heard that. He didn't want to be kept in quarantine. Not that he knew what it meant, but it sounded horrible.

'It's no big deal,' said Seb. 'It only means you'll get out of going to school and you won't be able to have any other children round. Because you might be infectious, see?'

Sally was lying in bed with tears in her eyes.

'Poor Smidge,' she said, 'you're going to be very lonely! Maybe we should ring Mum.'

But Miss Crawley wouldn't hear of it.

'Certainly not. Mrs Stevenson needs her peace and quiet. Remember she's ill as well. I shall look after that young man!'

She nodded in the direction of Smidge, who was standing by Sally's bed, his eyes all red with crying.

There wasn't time to say much more, because the ambulance came to pick up Seb and Sally. Smidge started crying again, because although his brother and sister made him very cross sometimes, he did like them a lot, and it was such a shame they had to go to hospital.

'Bye then, Smidge,' said Seb, as the ambulance men carted him off.

'Goodbye, little brother, and don't be sad!

We'll be home soon, you'll see,' said Sally.

Smidge howled.

'That's what you say! What if you both die?'

Miss Crawley told him off afterwards: how could he be so stupid as to think people died of scarlet fever?

Smidge went to his room. Bumble was waiting for him, and he scooped him up in his arms.

'Now I've only got you,' said Smidge, hugging Bumble. 'And Karlsson, of course.'

Bumble certainly seemed to understand that Smidge was upset. He licked his face. It was just as if he was trying to say:

'Yes, but at least you *have* got me. And Karlsson!'

Smidge sat there for a long time, thinking how wonderful it was having Bumble. But he was really missing Mum, even so. He remembered he had promised to write to her, and decided to do it straight away.

'Dear Mum,' he wrote,
'This family is braking up compleetly Seb and Sally have got scarlit fever and are in hospitel and I am in Kworenteen. It doesn't

hurt but I bet I'll get scarlit fever as well and Dad is in London if he is alive at all but I haven't heard he is ill but I bet he is becos all the others are. I reely miss you how are you anyway are you very poorly? There is a thing about Karlsson I ort to tell you but I wont becos you will only worry and you need peece and qiet said Creepy Crawley she isn't ill and nor is Karlsson tho I bet they soon will be. Goodbye, dear Mum, rest in peece!'

'I won't write any more,' Smidge told Bumble, 'because I don't want to scare her, after all.'

Then he went over to the window and rang for Karlsson. Yes, rang. Karlsson had done something very clever the evening before, you see. He had rigged up a bell system between his house on the roof and Smidge's room down below.

'You can't go out haunting just on the off-chance,' said Karlsson. 'But Karlsson has now wired up the world's best bell, so you can ring and order a haunting whenever Creepy Crawley sits herself down in some suitable spot and starts looking out into the night for scary little me.'

The system consisted of a cowbell fixed under the ridge of Karlsson's roof and a piece of string running from the cowbell down to Smidge's window.

'You pull the string,' said Karlsson, 'the bell rings up at my place, and hey presto, in flies your Neighbourhood Ghost, and Creepy Crawley has a fit, isn't that marvellous?'

Of course it was marvellous, and Smidge thought so too. But not just for haunting. Until now, he'd had to sit and wait until Karlsson felt like dropping in. Now he could ring for him whenever he needed to talk to him.

And Smidge really did feel he needed to talk to Karlsson, right now. He tugged and yanked at the string, and could hear the cowbell jangling away on the roof. Soon he heard the whirr of Karlsson's motor, too, but the Karlsson who came flying in at the window looked in rather a bad mood and as if he'd just woken up.

'Think this is meant as some sort of alarm clock?' he said peevishly.

'Oh, sorry,' said Smidge. 'Were you asleep?'

'You should have asked me that before you woke me up. You always sleep like a baby, you do, and you've no idea what it's like for us poor souls who hardly ever get a wink of sleep. When we do finally doze off, I think we might expect our friends to keep ever so totally quiet and hold their breaths instead of clanging bells as if there was a fire.'

'Do you have trouble sleeping, then?' said Smidge.

Karlsson nodded morosely.

'Yes I do, as a matter of fact.'

Smidge was sorry to hear it.

'You poor thing . . . do you really sleep badly?'

'Lousily,' said Karlsson. 'That's to say, I sleep

like a log at nights, and in the mornings, but it's the afternoons that are the worst, I just lie there tossing and turning.'

He stood quietly for a minute as if brooding about his sleep problems, but then he looked eagerly round the room.

'If someone gave me a little present, then I might not be quite so fed up that you woke me.'

Smidge didn't want Karlsson to be fed up, so he started hunting among his things.

'My mouth organ, would you like that?'

Karlsson snatched the mouth organ.

'Ooh, yes thanks, I've always wanted a musical instrument, I'll have this . . . unless you happen to have a double bass, that is.'

He put the mouth organ to his mouth and blew a few awful-sounding notes. He looked at Smidge and his eyes twinkled.

'Hear that? I've made up a nice, sad tune already. I call it "The Neighbourhood Ghost's Lament".'

Smidge said sad tunes were just right for this house full of ill people, and he told Karlsson all about the scarlet fever.

'Isn't it a shame for Seb and Sally?' he said.

But Karlsson said scarlet fever was a mere

trifle and nothing to worry about. As a matter of fact, it was rather handy having Seb and Sally away in hospital, now the big haunting was about to start.

No sooner had he said it than Smidge jumped with fright. He could hear Miss Crawley's steps outside the door and knew she would be barging into his room any second. Karlsson could see he had to do something quickly, too. He came in to land with a splat and rolled under Smidge's bed like a little ball. Smidge hastily sat down on the bed and spread his dressing gown over his knees, so it would hang down and hide as much of Karlsson as possible.

That moment the door opened and Miss Crawley stalked in with a dustpan and a broom.

'I'm going to clean up in here,' she said. 'You wait in the kitchen in the meantime!'

Smidge felt so nervous that he began to sweat.

'No, I don't want to,' he said. 'I'm supposed to stay in here and be in quarantine.'

Miss Crawley glared at him, annoyed.

'Do you know what you've got under your bed?' she asked.

Smidge went red in the face . . . had she spotted Karlsson?

'There . . . there isn't anything under my bed,' he stammered.

'Oh yes there is,' said Miss Crawley. 'There's a huge accumulation of fluff that I'm going to sweep up. Now move!'

Smidge was beside himself.

'No, I'm supposed to stay here and be in quarantine,' he cried.

So Miss Crawley, muttering, started to sweep the other end of the room.

'Well, sit there then, if you must, until I've finished over here. But then you'll have to be so kind as to be in quarantine in some other corner of the room, stubborn brat!'

Smidge chewed his nails and wondered how this was going to turn out. Then he gave a sudden start and began to giggle. Karlsson was tickling the back of his knee, and Smidge was *so* ticklish.

Miss Crawley glowered at him.

'Hark at you laughing, when your mother and brother and sister are all sick and suffering! Some people get over things very quickly, it seems to me.'

Again Smidge felt Karlsson tickling the back of his knee, and this time he had such a violent fit of the giggles that he almost fell off the bed.

'May I enquire what's so funny?' asked Miss Crawley tartly.

'Hee hee,' said Smidge, 'I've just remembered a joke . . . ' He racked his brains to think of one quickly.

'It's that one about the bull who charged at a horse, and the horse was so scared that he had to climb a tree. Have you heard it, Miss Crawley?'

Seb used to tell that joke sometimes, but Smidge had never laughed at it, because he felt so sorry for the poor horse, having to climb a tree.

Miss Crawley wasn't laughing, either.

'That's enough of your silly jokes. You know very well that horses can't climb trees.'

'No, they can't,' said Smidge, just like Seb usually did. 'But after all, he had an angry bull after him, so what the hell was he supposed to do?'

Seb had said you were *allowed* to say 'hell' when you were telling a joke that had the word 'hell' in. But Miss Crawley didn't agree. She looked disgustedly at Smidge.

'You sit here laughing and swearing, with your mother and brother and sister sick and suffering. I must say I'm staggered . . . '

She was interrupted right there. From under the bed came the sound of 'The Neighbourhood Ghost's Lament', just a few short, piercing notes, but enough to make Miss Crawley jump.

'What on earth was that?'

'*I* don't know,' said Smidge.

But Miss Crawley knew, oh yes!

'Those were sounds from another world, I'm absolutely sure of it.'

'From another world? What does that mean?' Smidge asked.

'From the world of ghosts,' said Miss Crawley. 'The only ones in this room are you and me, and neither of us can make sounds like that. That wasn't a human cry, it was a ghost's cry. Didn't you hear? It sounded like a soul in distress!'

She stared at Smidge, wide-eyed.

'Lordy lordy, I simply must write to the television people now.'

She threw down her dustpan and broom and sat herself at Smidge's desk. She found some paper and a pen. She wrote away busily for a long time. Then she read it all out to Smidge.

'Now just you listen to this!'

To Swedish Radio and Television.

My sister Frida Crawley was in your series about spirits and ghosts. I didn't think it was a very good programme, whatever Frida says. You need to do better than that, and here's a chance for you to do it, because I have ended up living in a real haunted house, and here's a list of all the hauntings I've had.

1. Strange mooing outside the window, and it can't have been a cow because we live on the fourth floor. It was just a sort of mooing.
2. Things vanishing mysteriously, such as buns, and little boys locked in rooms.
3. Doors that get locked from the outside while I'm inside, explain that if you can!

4. Ghastly ghost-writing on the kitchen wall.
5. Sudden funeral music while I was cleaning. Somehow made you want to cry.

Come at once, because this will really be a programme to get people talking.

Yours sincerely,

Hilda Crawley

P.S. Whatever gave you the idea of putting Frida on TV, of all people?

Then Miss Crawley, quite carried away, dashed out to post her letter. Smidge peered down at Karlsson. He was lying there under the bed with that glint in his eyes, and came wriggling out, as bright and cheerful as could be.

'Whoop, whoop!' he went. 'Just wait until it gets dark this evening. Miss Crawley's going to get something really worth writing to that television crowd about!'

Smidge started to giggle again, and gave Karlsson an affectionate look.

'It's fun being in quarantine as long as I can be in quarantine with you,' Smidge said.

He thought for a minute about Kris and Jemima, who he usually played with. He ought really to be feeling sad that he wouldn't be able to see them for quite a long time.

But it doesn't matter. It's more exciting playing with Karlsson, thought Smidge.

Only just now, Karlsson hadn't got time to play any more. He'd got to get home and mend his silencer, he said.

'We can't have the Neighbourhood Ghost flying in like a clattering dustbin, you know. Nope, it's got to be weird and silent and spooky enough to make Creepy Crawley's hair stand on end.'

Then Karlsson and Smidge decided on a special system of signals for their bell on a string.

'If you ring once,' said Karlsson, 'it means "Come straight away", and if you ring twice, it means "Don't come whatever you do", and three times means "Just imagine there being somebody in the world as handsome and perfectly plump and brave and great in every way as you, Karlsson".'

'Why would I want to ring you to say that?' asked Smidge.

'Well, because it's important to say kind and encouraging things to your friends every five minutes or so, and I can't be popping down here that often, you know.'

Smidge gave Karlsson a thoughtful look.

'I'm your friend, too, aren't I? But I don't think you ever say anything like that to me.'

Then Karlsson laughed.

'But that's different, obviously. You're just a silly little kid!'

Smidge nodded. He knew Karlsson was right.

'But you do like me, don't you?'

'Yes, of course,' Karlsson assured him. 'I don't quite know why I do, and I often brood about it when I'm lying there in the afternoons, not getting to sleep.'

He patted Smidge on the cheek.

'Certainly I like you, and there must be some reason for it . . . Maybe it's because you're so different from me, poor little chap!'

He flew up to the open window and waved goodbye.

'And if you ring wildly, as if there's a fire,' he said, 'it means either there *is* a fire, or "Now I've gone and woken you again, dear Karlsson, so bring a big bag and come and fetch all my toys . . . you can have them all as my way of saying sorry!"'

And Karlsson was gone.

But Bumble leapt onto the floor in front of Smidge and thumped his tail on the rug. It was his way of showing he really liked someone and wanted them to care about him. Smidge lay down on the floor beside him. That made Bumble jump up and bark with joy. Then he nestled up against Smidge's arm and shut his eyes.

'At least you think it's a good thing that I'm off school and in quarantine,' said Smidge. 'Bumble, *you* think I'm the world's best, don't you, boy?'

The Neighbourhood Ghost

Smidge had a long, lonely day, and he simply couldn't wait for the evening. It felt almost like a sort of Christmas Eve, he thought. He played with Bumble and looked through his stamp collection and did a few sums so he wouldn't get behind in class. And when it got to the time he thought Kris would be home from school, he rang him and told him about the scarlet fever.

'I can't come to school, because I'm in quarantine, you see.'

It sounded rather grand, he thought, and Kris must have thought so, too, because he went very quiet.

'You can tell Jemima, too,' said Smidge.

'Aren't you bored?' asked Kris when he finally found his tongue again.

'Oh no,' said Smidge. 'After all, I've got . . . '

He stopped. He had been going to say 'Karlsson', but Dad had told him not to. Although Kris and Jemima had bumped into Karlsson several times, back in the spring, that was *before* Dad said they mustn't tell a soul about him. Kris and Jemima would be sure to have forgotten about him by now, and that was just as well, Smidge thought.

Because that makes him my special, secret Karlsson, he thought. He quickly said goodbye to Kris.

'Bye then, I've got to go now.'

It was depressing eating dinner on his own with Miss Crawley, but she had made some very yummy meatballs. Smidge ate lots. For pudding she'd done apple cake and custard. That made him start to think she wasn't quite such a dead loss, after all.

The best thing about Miss Crawley is her apple cake, thought Smidge, and the best thing about the apple cake is the custard, and the best thing about the custard is that it's me eating it.

But dinnertime was still no fun at all, with so many empty places at the table. Smidge longed for Mum and Dad and Seb and Sally, one by one. No, it really wasn't any fun, and what was more, Miss Crawley would keep going on about Frida, and Smidge was already pretty tired of her.

But at last it was evening. It was autumn now, and it got dark earlier. Smidge stood at his window, pale with excitement, and watched the stars come out above the roofs. He waited. This was *worse* than Christmas Eve. You were only waiting for Father Christmas then, and what was that, compared to the Neighbourhood Ghost? Nothing! Smidge chewed his nails nervously. He knew Karlsson was waiting up there somewhere, too. Miss Crawley was sitting in the kitchen with her feet in a bowl of water. She was taking her daily footbath, but afterwards, she'd promised to come and say goodnight to Smidge. Then it would be time to ring the bell. And then . . . lordy lordy, as Miss Crawley always said . . . lordy lordy, this was exciting!

'If she doesn't come soon I shall burst,' muttered Smidge.

But here she was. In through the door strode Miss Crawley on big, newly washed, bare feet, making Smidge jump like a frightened little fish, even though he had been expecting her and knew she was coming.

Miss Crawley gave him a suspicious look.

'Why are you standing by the open window in your pyjamas? Get into bed.'

'I'm . . . I'm looking at the stars,' stammered Smidge. 'Wouldn't you like to have a look at them, too, Miss Crawley?'

That was his clever way of getting her over to the window. As he said it, he put his hand surreptitiously behind the curtain, where the string was, and gave it a hefty tug. He heard the bell ring, up on the roof. So did Miss Crawley.

'I can hear bells ringing up in space,' she said. 'How very odd!'

'Yes, that's strange,' said Smidge.

Then he held his breath. Because gliding down through the air from the roof came a white and rather roly-poly little ghost. It came with its own music. It sounded very faint and very sorrowful, but there was no mistaking the 'Neighbourhood Ghost's Lament' drifting across the autumn evening sky.

'There . . . just look there . . . oh lordy lordy!!' said Miss Crawley. She was as white as a sheet, and had to sit down on a chair. Even though she'd said she wasn't scared of ghosts!

Smidge tried to make her calm down.

'Yes, even I'm beginning to see ghosts now,' he said. 'But it's such a little ghost, it can't be dangerous.'

Miss Crawley wasn't listening. She was staring wild-eyed out at the sky, where the little ghost was showing off his flying stunts.

'Get rid of it! Get rid of it!' she gasped.

But there was no getting rid of the Neighbourhood Ghost. It floated one way and then the other, it soared and dived, and every so often it turned a somersault in mid-air. The mournful music just went on, even when the ghost was doing its somersaults.

It was really beautiful and poetic, thought Smidge: the little white ghost, the dark, starry sky, and the mournful music. But Miss Crawley didn't think so. She grabbed hold of Smidge.

'Let's run into the big bedroom and hide there!'

The Stevensons' flat had eight rooms, including the kitchen, hall, and bathroom. Seb, Sally, and Smidge had a small room each, Mum and Dad had the main bedroom, and then there was a large sitting room. While Mum and Dad were away, Miss Crawley was sleeping in their room. It faced the garden in the courtyard, while Smidge's window looked out over the street.

'Come on,' panted Miss Crawley, 'come on, we'll hide in the big bedroom!'

Smidge hung back. Surely they weren't going to run away from the haunting when it had only just started! But Miss Crawley was determined.

'Hurry up, before I faint clean away!'

So although Smidge didn't want to, he let himself be dragged off to the main bedroom. The window was open in there, too, but Miss Crawley rushed over and slammed it shut. She lowered the blinds and closed the curtains tight. Then she started piling furniture against the door for all she was worth. She was clearly ready to do anything in the world to avoid seeing another ghost. Smidge couldn't understand it; earlier on she'd been so keen to be haunted, hadn't she? He sat on Dad's bed, watching her toil away, and shook his head.

'Frida wouldn't get all worked up like that,' he said.

But Miss Crawley didn't want to hear a word about Frida just at the moment. She went on lugging bits of furniture: the chest of drawers and the table and all the chairs and a little bookcase. There was soon an impressive barricade in front of the door.

'Right, that's that,' said Miss Crawley, sounding satisfied. 'I think we can relax now.'

Then a deep voice, sounding even more satisfied, rang out from under Dad's bed:

'Right, that's that! I think we can relax now! We're shut in for the night now!'

And the Neighbourhood Ghost emerged with a whoosh.

'Help,' screamed Miss Crawley. 'Help!'

'How?' asked the ghost. 'Shift a bit of furniture, perhaps? I'm not a removal man, you know.'

The ghost laughed at its own words, long and loud. Miss Crawley didn't. She rushed to the door and started shoving aside bits of furniture, sending the chairs flying. She soon demolished the barricade and then launched herself into the hall, screaming at the top of her voice.

The ghost went after her. So did Smidge. Bringing up the rear came Bumble, barking wildly. He recognized the ghost from its smell, and thought it was a great game. The ghost plainly thought so, too.

'Whoop whoop!' it screeched, flapping round Miss Crawley's ears. But sometimes it let her get a bit ahead, to make it more exciting. They chased all round the flat, Miss Crawley in front and the Neighbourhood Ghost behind, into the kitchen and back out again, into the sitting room and back out again, into Smidge's room and back out again, round and round and round!

Miss Crawley screamed and shouted the whole way round, and in the end the ghost had to try to make her simmer down.

'Now now, don't howl like that! Just when we're having so much fun!'

But it was no use. Miss Crawley went on yelling and darted back into the kitchen. The bowl of water from her footbath was still standing on the floor. The ghost was right on her heels.

'Whoop, whoop!' it bawled in Miss Crawley's ear, and she fell over the bowl with a crash. She let out a booming roar, like a foghorn, and the ghost said:

'Sshhh! You'll frighten the life out of me and the neighbours. Calm down, or we'll have the police here.'

The floor was swimming in water, and in the middle of it all lay Miss Crawley. But she struggled to her feet with amazing speed and hared off, her wet skirt slapping soggily round her legs.

The ghost couldn't resist jumping up and down a few times in the water left in the bowl.

'Great for splashing the walls,' the ghost remarked to Smidge. 'Everybody enjoys a good trip over a bowl of water. What's she making such a fuss about?'

The ghost did one last jump and set off after Miss Crawley again. She was nowhere to be seen. But there were wet footmarks on the parquet floor in the hall.

'A trotting Creepy Crawley,' said the ghost. 'These are fresh tracks. We'll soon see where they lead. Because guess who's the world's best tracker dog!'

The tracks led to the bathroom. Miss Crawley had locked herself in, and they could hear her triumphant laughter echoing a long way.

The Neighbourhood Ghost knocked on the door. 'Open up, do you hear me!'

Another arrogant laugh rang out from the bathroom.

'Open the door . . . or you can count me out!' bellowed the ghost.

Miss Crawley had gone quiet, but she didn't open the door. The ghost turned to Smidge, who was trying to get his breath back after the chase.

'You tell her! It's no fun if she's going to be like this!'

Smidge gave a cautious knock on the door.

'It's only me, Miss Crawley,' he said. 'How long are you thinking of staying in the bathroom?'

'I'll be here all night, you can be sure of that,' said Miss Crawley. 'I'm just going to make up a bed in the bathtub with all the towels.'

Hearing that, the angry ghost retorted:

'Yes, go on then! Just spoil everything, so we can't have *any* fun any more! But if you do, guess who'll be off to haunt Frida?'

It went very quiet for a while inside the bathroom. Miss Crawley was presumably sitting thinking over this awful threat. But eventually she said in a pitiful, pleading little voice:

'No, don't do that, eh? I . . . I don't think you should!'

'All right, you come out then,' said the ghost. 'Or I'm straight off to Frey Street. And then we'll have Frida on the TV box again, sure as eggs is eggs.'

They heard Miss Crawley sigh several times. In the end she called out:

'Smidge, put your ear to the keyhole. I want to whisper something to you.'

Smidge did as she asked. He put his ear to the keyhole, and Miss Crawley whispered to him:

'I thought I wasn't afraid of ghosts, you see,

but I am. You're so brave, can't you ask that dreadful creature to go away and come back another time, when I've got a bit more used to the idea? But to *not* go to Frida's in the meantime. He's got to promise that!'

'I'll see what I can do,' said Smidge. He turned round to speak to the ghost. But the ghost wasn't there.

'He's gone,' shouted Smidge. 'He must have gone home. Do come out!'

But Miss Crawley didn't dare come out until Smidge had searched the whole flat to make sure the ghost had gone.

Then Miss Crawley sat in Smidge's room for a long time, shaking all over. But eventually she recovered, and was surprisingly perky.

'Ooh, it was dreadful while it lasted,' she said. 'But just think, *just think* what a TV programme this will make! Frida's never seen anything to compare with this.'

She sat there looking forward to it, as happy as a babe in arms. Just occasionally she gave a shudder as she remembered the ghostly chase they'd had.

'To be honest, I think that's quite enough

haunting for now,' she said. 'I hope I never have to see that nasty customer again!'

She had scarcely finished speaking before they heard a low mooing from Smidge's wardrobe, and that was quite enough to send Miss Crawley into hysterics again.

'Did you hear that? Mark my words, we've got the ghost in the wardrobe now . . . oh, I think I'm going to die.'

Smidge felt sorry for her, but he didn't know what to say to comfort her.

'Oh no,' he said. 'That's not a ghost . . . perhaps it's a little cow . . . yes, let's hope it's a little cow.'

But then a voice came from the wardrobe:

'A little cow indeed! Well, it isn't, so there!'

The wardrobe door opened, and out came the Neighbourhood Ghost in the white costume Smidge had made for it. It rose into the air with deep, ghostly sighs and started circling round the ceiling light in short little sweeps.

'Whoop, whoop, the world's most dangerous ghost, *not* a little cow!'

Miss Crawley screamed. Round and round flew the ghost, faster and faster it went, and

Miss Crawley's screams rose louder and louder as the ghost grew wilder and wilder.

But then something happened. The ghost banked a little too sharply, and its costume caught on a pointy bit of the light.

There was a 'Rrripp!' as the worn old sheets tore, the ghost outfit slipped off and was left hanging there, and Karlsson was left flying round the light in his ordinary blue trousers, checked shirt, and red-and-white striped socks. He was so carried away that he didn't even notice. He just kept flying round and round, wailing and moaning more spookily than ever. But on his fourth circuit, he finally saw there was something hanging from the light, fluttering in the draught as he zoomed by.

'What's this cloth you've got dangling from your light?' he said. 'Is it some kind of fly net?'

Smidge could only groan:

'No, Karlsson, it's not a fly net.'

Then Karlsson looked down at his tubby self, saw the problem, saw his blue trousers, saw he was no longer the Neighbourhood Ghost but just plain Karlsson.

He landed in front of Smidge with an

embarrassed little thud.

'Ho hum,' he said, 'accidents happen to the best of us, as we've just seen . . . but ho hum, it's a mere trifle, anyway!'

Miss Crawley sat staring at him, white in the face. She was gasping for air like a fish on dry land. Finally she managed to get out a few words.

'Who . . . who . . . oh lordy lordy, who is that?'

And Smidge said, with a sob in his voice:

'It's Karlsson on the Roof.'

'And who,' panted Miss Crawley, 'is Karlsson on the Roof?'

Karlsson gave a bow.

'A handsome, thoroughly clever, perfectly plump man in his prime, I am, so there!'

Not a Ghost,
Just Plain Karlsson

It turned out to be an evening Smidge would never forget. Miss Crawley sat on a chair, crying, and Karlsson kept well away from her, looking almost ashamed of himself. Nobody said anything; it was all a big mess.

This is enough to give me lines on my forehead, thought Smidge, because that was what Mum sometimes said. It was like when Seb came home the day he'd failed three subjects at once, or when Sally kept nagging about wanting a fur jacket just when Dad had the new television set to pay for, or when Smidge threw stones in the school playground and broke a window. Then Mum had sighed and said, 'This is enough to give me lines on my forehead!'

That was exactly how Smidge felt now. Oh dear, how horrible everything was! Miss Crawley was crying buckets of tears. And why? Just because Karlsson wasn't a ghost.

'That's my ghost programme gone up in smoke,' she said, glaring at Karlsson. 'And just when I'd said to Frida . . . '

She buried her face in her hands and cried so loudly that nobody could hear what she'd said to Frida.

'But I really am a handsome, thoroughly clever, perfectly plump man in his prime, you know,' Karlsson said, trying to console her. 'I wouldn't mind coming along and being in that box . . . maybe with some little princess or other!'

Miss Crawley took her hands away from her face and looked at Karlsson. She gave a scornful snort.

'Handsome, clever, perfectly plump man, that's just the sort of thing to interest them when TV's already full of them!'

She gave Karlsson a cross and mistrusting

look . . . that little fatso, he must be a boy, mustn't he, even though he looked like a small man? She asked Smidge:

'Who is this character, tell me that.'

And Smidge answered truthfully:

'He's someone I play with.'

'I thought as much,' said Miss Crawley.

Then she started crying again. Smidge was amazed. There were Mum and Dad, thinking that if anybody ever caught a glimpse of Karlsson there'd be a huge hullabaloo and everyone would come rushing and want to put him on television. But the only person who actually *had* seen Karlsson was crying and saying he was worthless, because he wasn't a ghost. The fact that he had a propeller and could fly didn't impress her at all.

Karlsson was at that moment flying up to unhook his ghost outfit from the light, but Miss Crawley just glowered at him more crossly than ever and said:

'Propellers and gadgets and I don't know what else. All the things kids expect these days! Suppose they'll be flying to the moon soon, before they've even started school!'

She sat there getting crosser and crosser, as she started to realize exactly who had pinched the buns, as well, and mooed outside the window and written the ghost-writing on the kitchen wall. Fancy giving children gadgets that meant they could fly about and tease old folk like that! All the hauntings she'd written about to the television company were nothing but boys' pranks, and she couldn't bear looking at that fat little good-for-nothing a minute longer.

'Get off home, you there, whatever you're called!'

'Karlsson,' said Karlsson.

'I know that,' said Miss Crawley in exasperation, 'but surely you've got a first name, too?'

'Karlsson's my first name and my surname,' said Karlsson.

'Don't you provoke me and make me cross, because I already am,' said Miss Crawley. 'First names, they're what people *call* you, don't you know that? What does your father call you when he wants you for something?'

'Little devil,' said Karlsson smugly.

Miss Crawley nodded approvingly.

'He never said a truer word, your father!'

And Karlsson agreed with her.

'Oh yes, when I was little, I certainly was a little devil then! But that was a long time ago. These days, I'm the world's best-behaved Karlsson!'

But Miss Crawley wasn't listening any longer. She was sitting quietly, thinking things over, and seemed to be calming down a bit.

'Well,' she said at last. 'I know one person who'll be pleased about all this, at any rate.'

'Who,' asked Smidge.

'Frida,' said Miss Crawley bitterly. Then she vanished into the kitchen with a sigh, to mop up all the water and put the bowl away.

Karlsson and Smidge thought it was nice to be on their own.

'What a fuss some people make about little things,' said Karlsson, and shrugged. 'What have I ever done to her, eh?'

'Nothing,' said Smidge. 'Only tirritated her a bit, perhaps. But we'd better behave ourselves now.'

Karlsson thought so too.

'Of course we'll behave! I'm *always* the world's best-behaved Karlsson. But I have to have some fun, otherwise you can count me out.'

Smidge thought about it and tried to come up with something Karlsson would enjoy. But he didn't need to, because Karlsson did it for himself. He rushed into Smidge's wardrobe.

'Hang on, I saw a funny thing in here when I was a ghost.'

He came out clutching a little mousetrap. Smidge had found it when he was staying in the country at Granny's, and brought it back to Stockholm with him.

'Because I really would like to catch a mouse and tame her and have her as a pet,' Smidge had explained to Mum. Mum said city flats didn't have mice, thank goodness, or theirs didn't, anyway. Smidge told Karlsson this, but Karlsson said:

'A mouse nobody knows about might come along. A little surprise mouse who comes pattering in, just to make your mum happy.'

Karlsson told Smidge how great it would be if they could catch that surprise mouse, because then he could keep her up in his house on the roof, and if she had babies, he'd eventually have a whole mouse farm.

'And then I'll put an advert in the paper,'

said Karlsson. 'If it's mice you need, then ring Karlsson's mouse farm right away!'

'Yes, and then even city flats can have mice,' said Smidge happily. He showed Karlsson how to set the trap.

'But you have to have a piece of cheese or bacon rind in it, of course, or no mouse will come.'

Karlsson put his hand in his back pocket and pulled out a little bit of bacon rind.

'It's just as well I saved this at dinnertime, instead of throwing it down the rubbish chute.'

He hooked the bacon rind into place and put the mousetrap under Smidge's bed.

'There! Now the mouse can come whenever she likes.'

They had almost forgotten Miss Crawley. But at that moment they heard her bashing about in the kitchen.

'It sounds as if she's cooking something,' said Karlsson. 'She's making frying pan noises.'

And he was right. There was soon a delicious smell of meatballs finding its way out of the kitchen.

'She's frying the meatballs left over from

dinner,' said Smidge. 'Oh, it makes me feel hungry!'

Karlsson dashed to the door.

'Off to the kitchen with a leap and a bound!' he cried.

Smidge thought Karlsson was very brave, daring to go in there, but he didn't want to let the side down, either. He followed cautiously.

Karlsson was already in the kitchen.

'Whoop, whoop, I think we're just in time for a light supper.'

Miss Crawley was standing at the stove, shaking the pan of meatballs, but when she saw Karlsson she put it down and came towards him. She looked cross and threatening.

'Get lost,' she shouted. 'Out with you, right now!'

Karlsson's mouth drooped and he put on his sulky look.

'You can count me out, if you're going to be such a sourpuss. I'm entitled to some meatballs too, aren't I? Don't you realize how hungry it makes you, zooming around haunting all evening?'

He dodged towards the stove and snatched a

meatball from the frying pan. But he shouldn't have done that. Miss Crawley let out a roar and came straight for him. She picked him up by the scruff of his neck and dumped him outside the kitchen door.

'Get lost,' she screeched. 'Go home and don't stick your nose in here again!'

Smidge was absolutely furious, and in utter despair . . . how could anybody do that to his beloved Karlsson?

'How can you be so horrible?' he said, feeling the tears welling up in his throat. 'Karlsson's my friend and he's *allowed* to be here.'

He got no further before the kitchen door opened. In stomped Karlsson, and he was hopping mad, too.

'You can count me out,' he shouted. 'You can count me out, if this is how it's going to be! Think you can throw me out of the back door like that, then count me out, that's all!'

He went up to Miss Crawley and stamped his foot on the floor.

'The back door, ugh! I want to be thrown out of the front door like other posh people!'

Miss Crawley grabbed the scruff of his

neck again.

'By all means,' she said, and despite Smidge running after her, crying and protesting, she carted Karlsson off through the flat and heaved him out of the front door, so he got what he wanted.

'There,' she said. 'Is that posh enough for you?'

'Yes, that's fine,' said Karlsson, and Miss Crawley slammed the door behind him with such force that the whole building shook.

'At last,' she said, and marched back to the kitchen.

Smidge ran after her, arguing.

'Oh come on, that's really mean and unfair! Of course Karlsson's allowed in the kitchen.'

And he was, too! When Miss Crawley and Smidge got there, Karlsson was standing by the stove, eating meatballs.

'Yes, I want to be thrown out of the front door, naturally, so I can come back in through the back door and get myself some yummy meatballs.'

Then Miss Crawley picked him up by the scruff of his neck and threw him out for the third time, this time the back way.

'This is getting ridiculous,' she said. 'You're

a bad penny, and no mistake! But if I lock the door, then maybe we'll be rid of you at last.'

'We'll have to see about that,' said Karlsson mildly.

The door closed behind him, and Miss Crawley made sure it was properly locked.

'You really are being horrible,' said Smidge. But she wasn't listening. She was on her way to the stove, where the meatballs were sizzling appetizingly in the pan.

'Maybe I can finally have a meatball myself, after all I've had to put up with this evening,' she said.

Then they heard a voice from the open window.

'Good evening, anyone at home? And are there any meatballs left?'

And there sat Karlsson on the window ledge, beaming at them. Smidge burst out laughing.

'Did you fly over from the balcony?'

Karlsson nodded.

'Certainly did. So here I am again. Expect everybody's glad about that . . . especially you over there by the stove!'

Miss Crawley was poised with a meatball

in her hand. She had been about to pop it into her mouth, but when she saw Karlsson she just stood there, gaping.

'Never seen such a greedy girl,' said Karlsson, and dived down on her. He snatched the meatball as he zipped past, and flew briskly up to the ceiling.

But then Miss Crawley snapped back into action. She let out a little shriek, grabbed a carpet beater and ran after Karlsson with it.

'You wretched mischief-maker, I'll drive you out, you see if I don't!'

Karlsson jubilantly circled the ceiling light.

'Whoop, whoop, time for another tussle!' he shouted. 'I haven't enjoyed myself this much since I was little and Dad chased me for miles round Lake Mälaren with a fly swatter, whoop, whoop, we did have fun!'

Karlsson whizzed out into the hall, and a mad chase around the flat followed. First came Karlsson in mid-air, chuckling and hooting with delight, then Miss Crawley with the carpet beater, then Smidge, and finally a wildly barking Bumble.

'Whoop, whoop!' went Karlsson.

Miss Crawley was right behind Karlsson, but whenever she got too close, Karlsson put on a burst of speed and soared up to the ceiling. And however Miss Crawley brandished the carpet beater, she never managed to do more than brush the soles of his boots.

'Naughty naughty,' said Karlsson. 'No tickling my feet. That's against the rules. Watch it, or you'll have to count me out!'

Miss Crawley puffed as she ran, and her big, broad feet pounded on the parquet floor. The poor woman hadn't even had time to get her stockings and shoes back on, what with all the haunting and chasing they'd had that evening. She was getting exhausted, but she wouldn't give up.

'Just you wait!' she cried, still in hot pursuit. Every so often she leapt into the air to try to reach Karlsson with the carpet beater, but he just roared with laughter and dodged aside. Smidge was laughing too; he couldn't help it. He laughed so hard that he made his tummy ache, and as they charged through his room for the third time, he collapsed onto his bed for a little rest. He lay there, quite worn out, but still couldn't help giggling as he watched Miss Crawley chasing Karlsson round the flat.

'Whoop, whoop!' cried Karlsson.

'I'll give you whoop, whoop,' puffed Miss Crawley. She wielded the carpet beater furiously and finally managed to drive Karlsson into a corner, by Smidge's bed.

'Hah!' shouted Miss Crawley. 'I've got you now!'

Then she let out such a howl that it quite deafened Smidge. He stopped giggling.

Oh no, he thought. He's trapped!

But it wasn't Karlsson who was trapped. It was Miss Crawley. She'd got her big toe caught in the mousetrap.

'Ow,' cried Miss Crawley. 'Owwww!'

She pulled her foot out from under the bed and stared dumbstruck at the peculiar object dangling from her big toe.

'Oh no!' said Smidge. 'Hang on, I'll get it off for you . . . oops, sorry, I didn't mean to do that!'

'Owwww!' repeated Miss Crawley, once Smidge had helped her get free and she finally found her tongue. '*Why* have you got a mousetrap under your bed?'

Smidge felt genuinely sorry for her, and stammered desperately:

'Because . . . because . . . we wanted to catch a surprise mouse in it.'

'But not quite such a big one,' said Karlsson. 'More of a sweet little one with a long tail.'

Miss Crawley eyed Karlsson and groaned. 'You . . . you . . . are getting out *right now!*'

And she set off after him with the carpet beater, all over again.

'Whoop, whoop!' shouted Karlsson. He flew out into the hall, and off they raced again, into the sitting room and out again, into the kitchen and out again, into the big bedroom . . .

'Whoop, whoop!' went Karlsson.

'I'll give you whoop, whoop,' puffed Miss Crawley, and launched herself into an extra-high leap to swat him with the carpet beater. But she'd forgotten all the pieces of furniture she'd abandoned just inside the bedroom door, and as she jumped she tripped head over heels over the little bookcase and landed with a crash on the floor.

'Oops, I bet this is going to mean another earthquake in northern Norrland,' said Karlsson.

But Smidge rushed anxiously over to Miss Crawley.

'Are you all right?' he asked. 'Oh, poor Miss Crawley!'

'Help me onto the bed,' Miss Crawley managed to say.

And that's what Smidge did, or at least, he tried. But Miss Crawley was so big and heavy, and Smidge was so small, he couldn't do it. Then Karlsson came flying down.

'Now hang on,' he said to Smidge. 'I want to be in on the lugging too, you know. Seeing as it's me who's the kindest person in the world, not you!'

The two of them really put their backs into it, Karlsson and Smidge, and they finally managed to heave Miss Crawley into bed.

'Poor Miss Crawley,' said Smidge. 'How are you feeling? Does it hurt anywhere?'

Miss Crawley lay there and considered the matter.

'Well, I'm sure I haven't an unbroken bone left in my body,' she said finally, 'but it doesn't actually hurt anywhere . . . or only if I laugh!'

And then she began laughing so much that

the whole bed shook.

Smidge looked at her in alarm. What was the matter with her?

'Say what you like,' said Miss Crawley. 'I've run a couple of good marathons this evening, and lordy lordy how they pep you up!'

She nodded energetically.

'Just wait! Frida and I go to keep fit classes, and you wait for the next session, I'll show Frida someone who can really run!'

'Whoop, whoop!' said Karlsson. 'Take the carpet beater with you, and you can chase Frida all round the gym and pep her up too.'

Miss Crawley glared at him.

'Be quiet when you're talking to me! Shut up and go and fetch me some meatballs!'

Smidge laughed delightedly.

'Yes, running really gives you an appetite,' he said.

'And guess who's the world's best meatball fetcher,' said Karlsson. He was already halfway to the kitchen.

Then Karlsson and Smidge and Miss Crawley had a lovely little supper, sitting on the edge of the bed. Karlsson came back from the kitchen with a loaded tray.

'I saw there was some apple cake and custard, so I brought that too. And a bit of ham and cheese and salami and some pickled gherkins and a few sardines and a bit of liver pâté, but where in the world have you hidden the cream cake?'

'There is no cream cake,' said Miss Crawley.

The corners of Karlsson's mouth drooped.

'So we're meant to get full up on a few meatballs and apple cake and custard and ham and cheese and salami and gherkins and a couple of mangy sardines, are we?'

Miss Crawley looked him straight in the eye.

'No,' she said firmly. 'There's liver pâté too, you know.'

Smidge couldn't remember food ever having tasted so good. And they had such a nice time, he and Karlsson and Miss Crawley, sitting there the three of them, munching away. But all of a sudden Miss Crawley cried:

'Lordy lordy, Smidge is meant to be in quarantine, and we've gone and let that one in!'

She pointed at Karlsson.

'No, we didn't let him in. He came in by himself,' said Smidge. But he was still worried.

'Hey, Karlsson, what if you were to get scarlet fever now?'

'Um . . . um . . . ' said Karlsson, who had his mouth full of apple cake, and couldn't answer for a while.

'Scarlet fever . . . whoop, whoop! Anyone who's had the world's worst case of bun fever and lived to tell the tale can survive anything.'

'Bother, that didn't work either,' said Miss Crawley with a sigh.

Karlsson popped the last meatball into his mouth, then licked his fingers and said:

'I don't think much of the portions in this house, but I like it here otherwise. So perhaps I'll put myself in quarantine here, too.'

'Heaven preserve us,' said Miss Crawley.

She glowered at Karlsson, and at the tray, which was entirely empty of food.

'Not many leftovers when you come round, are there?' she said.

Karlsson got to his feet. He patted his tummy. 'When I've finished, I leave the table,' he said. 'But that's the only thing I leave.'

Then he turned his winder, his motor began to whirr, and he flew heavily towards the open window.

'Heysan hopsan,' he cried. 'You'll have to manage without me for a while, I'm in a rush now!'

'Heysan hopsan, Karlsson,' said Smidge. 'Have you really got to go?'

'So soon,' said Miss Crawley grimly.

'Yes, I've got to hurry now,' cried Karlsson. 'Otherwise I'll be late for my evening meal. Whoop, whoop!'

And he was gone.

Noble Maiden
Takes to the Air

The next day, Smidge slept in. He was woken by the ringing of the telephone, and rushed into the hall to answer. It was Mum.

'My darling Smidge . . . how dreadful!'

'What is?' asked Smidge sleepily.

'All those things you wrote in your letter. I've been so worried.'

'Why?' asked Smidge.

'Oh, you know very well,' said Mum. 'Poor little chap . . . but I'm coming home tomorrow.'

Smidge felt happy and wide awake, all at once.

But he didn't understand why Mum was calling him 'poor little chap'.

Smidge had no sooner hung up than the phone rang again. It was Dad, ringing all the way from London.

'How are you?' asked Dad. 'Are Seb and Sally being nice?'

'I shouldn't think so,' replied Smidge. 'But I can't say for sure, because they're in hospital.'

He could hear how worried this news made Dad. 'In hospital, whatever do you mean?'

And once Smidge had explained, Dad said exactly the same as Mum.

'Poor little chap . . . I'm coming home tomorrow.'

That was the end of the call. But straight away the phone rang again. This time it was Seb.

'You can tell Creepy Crawley and her old doctor that whatever they're experts in, it isn't scarlet fever. Sally and I are coming home tomorrow.'

'Haven't you got scarlet fever, then?' asked Smidge.

'No, we jolly well haven't. We've had too much hot chocolate and buns, the doctor here says. That can give you a rash if you're specially sensitive.'

'A clear case of bun fever, then,' said Smidge.

But Seb had already rung off.

As soon as Smidge was dressed, he went out to the kitchen to tell Miss Crawley his quarantine was over.

She had already started preparing lunch. The whole kitchen smelt of spices.

'Fine by me,' said Miss Crawley, once Smidge had explained that the whole family would be coming home. 'It'll be just as well for me to leave this job before my nerves are totally frayed.'

She was violently stirring the contents of a saucepan on the stove. She had some kind of thick stew in it, and was seasoning it generously with salt, pepper, and curry powder.

'There,' she said. 'You have to put plenty of salt and pepper and curry in this, to make it taste really good!'

Then she glanced uneasily at Smidge.

'You don't think that dreadful Karlsson will be coming again today, do you? It would be nice if my last hours here could be a bit more peaceful.'

Before Smidge had time to answer, a cheery voice outside the window sang at top volume:

'The sun has got his hat on,
hip hip hip hooray!
The sun has got his hat on
and he's coming out today.'

It was Karlsson, perched on the window ledge.

'Heysan hopsan, here comes your little sunbeam. Now we can have some fun.'

But Miss Crawley held up her hands imploringly.

'Oh no! No, anything but more of your fun!'

'Well, we'll be eating first, of course,' said Karlsson, and skipped over to the kitchen table. Miss Crawley had laid places for herself and Smidge. Karlsson sat down at one of them and seized the knife and fork.

'Look sharp! Bring on the food!'

He gave Miss Crawley a friendly nod.

'It's all right for you to sit at the table, too. Bring yourself a plate!'

Then he sniffed the air. 'What are we having?'

'A slice of humble pie and a good hiding,' said Miss Crawley, stirring her stew even more frantically. 'That's what *you* could do with, anyway, but I'm so stiff all over that I'm afraid I won't be doing any running today.'

She put the stew into a serving dish and brought it to the table. 'You two get on with yours,' she said, 'but I shall have mine afterwards. The doctor's told me I need peace and quiet when I'm eating.'

Karlsson nodded.

'Well, I expect there are a few dry biscuits in a tin somewhere that you can nibble, once we've polished off this lot . . . you have your little crust in peace and quiet, that's fine by us!'

And he ladled a huge helping onto his plate. But Smidge only took a little. He was always wary of food he didn't recognize. And he had never seen a stew like this before.

Karlsson started by piling all his stew into a tall mound, with a moat round it. While he was busy doing that, Smidge took his first cautious bite . . . oh! He gasped and tears came into his eyes. His whole mouth was on fire. But Miss

Crawley was standing there looking at him expectantly, so he swallowed and said nothing.

Then Karlsson looked up from his mound-making.

'What's up with you? Why are you crying?'

'I . . . I just happened to think of something tragic,' stammered Smidge.

'Ah, I see,' said Karlsson, and attacked his mound with a healthy appetite. But as soon as he had swallowed the first mouthful, he gave a yelp and his eyes filled with tears.

'What is it?' asked Miss Crawley.

'Rat poison, I think . . . but you should know, it's your concoction,' said Karlsson. 'Quick, bring the fire extinguisher, my throat's burning up.'

He wiped the tears from his eyes.

'What are you crying for?' asked Smidge.

'I happened to think of something tragic, too,' said Karlsson.

'What was it?' asked Smidge.

'This stew,' said Karlsson.

But that didn't please Miss Crawley at all.

'You kids should be ashamed of yourselves! There are thousands of children in this world who'd give anything for a stew like this.'

Karlsson stuck his hand in his pocket and produced a notebook and pencil.

'Give me the names and addresses of two of them,' he demanded.

But Miss Crawley just muttered and refused to say.

'They must be fire-eaters' children, the lot of them,' said Karlsson, 'brought up on a diet of fire and brimstone.'

Just then there was a ring at the front door, and Miss Crawley went to answer.

'Let's go with her and see who it is,' said Karlsson. 'It might be one of the thousand fire-eaters' children coming and wanting to give anything for her fire porridge, and if it is, we need to make sure she doesn't sell it too cheap . . . when you think of all the expensive rat poison she must have chucked in there!'

He went after Miss Crawley, and Smidge did too. They were standing right behind her when she opened the door, and they heard a voice outside say:

'My name's Peck. I'm from Swedish Radio and Television.'

Smidge felt himself go cold. He peeped

cautiously out from behind Miss Crawley's skirts, and there stood a gentleman, clearly one of those handsome, thoroughly clever, perfectly plump men in their prime who Miss Crawley said there were so many of on television.

'Could I speak to Miss Hilda Crawley, please?' asked Mr Peck.

'That's me,' said Miss Crawley. 'But I've paid my TV licence, so don't get any ideas!'

Mr Peck gave her a friendly smile.

'I'm not here about your licence. No, it's those hauntings you wrote to us about . . . we'd rather like to make a programme about them.'

Miss Crawley blushed bright red. She didn't say a word.

'What's the matter, aren't you feeling well?' Mr Peck eventually enquired.

'No,' said Miss Crawley. 'I'm not feeling well. This is the worst moment of my life.'

Smidge, standing right behind her, felt much the same thing. Lordy lordy, the game was really up now! Any second, Mr Peck would see Karlsson, and by the time Mum and Dad got home tomorrow, the whole house would be full of cables and television cameras and perfectly plump men and not a moment's peace and quiet. Oh lordy lordy, how could he smuggle Karlsson out of sight?

Then his eye fell on the old wooden chest standing in the hall. Sally used it for all her dressing up stuff. She and her classmates had some silly club, and sometimes they met at Sally's and dressed up and wandered round pretending to be totally different people—it was called drama and it was pretty stupid, Smidge thought. But oh, what a good job the chest was there just now. Smidge opened the lid and said to Karlsson in a nervous whisper:

'Hurry up . . . hide in this chest!'

And though Karlsson had no idea *why* he had to hide, he wasn't one to refuse if there was the chance of a bit of jiggery-pokery. He gave Smidge a sly wink and leapt into the chest. Smidge promptly shut the lid. He glanced anxiously at the two by the door . . . had they noticed anything?

They hadn't. Mr Peck and Miss Crawley were trying to get to the bottom of why Miss Crawley didn't feel well.

'They weren't hauntings,' said Miss Crawley,

on the verge of tears. 'They were just wretched boys' tricks, the lot of them.'

'So you weren't being haunted, then?' said Mr Peck.

Then Miss Crawley start crying in earnest.

'No, I wasn't being haunted . . . and now I'll never be on TV . . . only Frida!'

Mr Peck gave her a comforting pat on the arm. 'Please don't take it so hard, Miss Crawley. Perhaps one day you will, in some other context.'

'No I won't,' said Miss Crawley. She sank down onto the drama chest and covered her face in her hands. There she sat, weeping. Smidge felt so sorry for her, and ashamed that the whole thing was his fault.

Then there was a low rumbling sound from the chest.

'Oh, sorry,' said Miss Crawley. 'It's only because I'm so hungry.'

'Ah, that's stomachs for you,' said Mr Peck kindly. 'But your lunch must be virtually ready, I can smell something nice. What's cooking?'

'Just a stew,' sobbed Miss Crawley. 'It's my own invention . . . "Hilda's Spicy Special", I call it.'

'It smells wonderful,' said Mr Peck. 'Enough to make your mouth water.'

Miss Crawley got up from the chest.

'Well, you're welcome to sample it, because these little monkeys won't eat it.'

Mr Peck said he couldn't possibly and it wouldn't be right, but in the end he and Miss Crawley went off to the kitchen together.

Smidge lifted the lid of the chest and looked at Karlsson, who was lying there, rumbling gently.

'Stay in there until he's gone, for goodness' sake,' said Smidge, 'or you'll end up in the TV box.'

'Humph,' said Karlsson. 'This box is a tight squeeze too, let me tell you.'

So Smidge propped the chest lid a bit open to give Karlsson some air, and dashed off to the kitchen. He wanted to see Mr Peck's face when he tried Miss Crawley's Spicy Special.

But guess what? Mr Peck was at the table, gobbling it up as if it was the tastiest dish he'd ever tried. He had no tears in his eyes at all. But Miss Crawley did. Not from the stew, of course, but because she was still crying about her ghost programme that had come to nothing. It didn't help that Mr Peck was a big fan of her fire porridge; she was still upset.

But then something incredible happened. Mr Peck suddenly announced out of nowhere:

'I've got it! You can be on tomorrow evening.'

Miss Crawley looked at him, red-eyed.

'Be on what?' she asked glumly.

'On television, of course,' said Mr Peck. 'In our "My Best Recipe" slot. You can show the whole of Sweden how to make "Hilda's Spicy Special".'

There was a thud. Miss Crawley had fainted.

But she soon came round and hauled herself up off the floor. Her eyes were shining.

'Tomorrow evening . . . on TV, you say? My Spicy Special . . . you want me to make it for the whole of Sweden? Lordy lordy . . . And just think, Frida, she's absolutely clueless about cooking, and she calls my Spicy Special "chicken feed"!'

Smidge was totally engrossed; this was very interesting. He'd almost forgotten about Karlsson in the chest. But now, to his horror, he heard someone coming across the hall.

And sure enough, it was Karlsson! The door
between the hall and the kitchen was open, and
Smidge could see him coming, long before Miss
Crawley or Mr Peck noticed anything.

Yes, it was Karlsson! And yet it wasn't—
lordy lordy, what did he look like, all dressed
up in Sally's old drama costume, with a long
velvet skirt dragging round his legs and gauzy
veils hanging down back and front. He looked
more like a cheery little old lady than anything
else. And the cheery little old lady was
approaching doggedly. Smidge gestured wildly

to make Karlsson realize he mustn't come in. But Karlsson didn't seem to understand . . . and in he came.

'Noble maiden she enters the king's high hall,' said Karlsson.

And there he stood in the doorway, with his veils and everything. It was a vision that made Mr Peck's eyes pop out on stalks.

'Who on earth . . . ? Who's this funny little girl?' he said.

Miss Crawley couldn't contain herself.

'Funny little girl? No, the most appalling young scamp of a boy I've ever met in my life. Get out of here, you horrible child!'

But Karlsson wasn't listening.

'Noble maiden she dances, and her heart is glad,' he said.

And he began a dance. Smidge had never seen anything like it, and it didn't look as if Mr Peck had, either.

Karlsson shimmied round the room, his legs strangely bent at the knee. From time to time he did little leaps and waved his veils.

It looks totally weird, thought Smidge. But as long as he doesn't start flying, I suppose it doesn't matter. Oh, I hope he won't!

Karlsson had so many veils draped round him that you couldn't see his propeller. Smidge was glad of that. But what if Karlsson suddenly took off? Mr Peck would have a fit, and then be rushing here with his TV cameras as soon as he came to his senses again.

Mr Peck was watching the strange dance and laughing. He laughed more and more. That made Karlsson giggle, too, and flutter his eyelashes at Mr Peck as he shimmied past and waved the veils at him.

'Rather amusing boy,' said Mr Peck. 'We could have him on one of our children's programmes.'

He couldn't have said anything to infuriate Miss Crawley more.

'Put *him* on TV? In that case I'd rather not be there. Though obviously if you want someone to turn your studios upside down, then there's no better choice than him.'

Smidge nodded. 'And once he's turned the studios upside down, he'll say it's a mere trifle, you have to watch him!'

Mr Peck didn't insist.

'On second thoughts . . . it was only an idea!

And there are so many other youngsters, after all.'

Mr Peck was in a hurry now, anyway, because he had to get to a recording. He was just about to go. Then Smidge saw Karlsson start to feel for his winder. He had trouble getting to it, because of all the veils.

Mr Peck had already reached the door . . . when Karlsson's motor whirred into life.

'I didn't know the airport flight path went over this part of Stockholm,' Mr Peck said. 'They really should do something about it. Goodbye, Miss Crawley, see you tomorrow.'

And he went. But Karlsson rose to the ceiling and waved his veils at Miss Crawley.

'Noble maiden, she takes to the air, whoop, whoop!' he said.

Handsome, Thoroughly Clever, and Perfectly Plump . . .

Smidge spent all that afternoon up at Karlsson's house on the roof. He'd explained to Karlsson why they really must leave Miss Crawley in peace.

'She's making a cream cake, you know, for when Mum and Dad and Seb and Sally come home tomorrow.'

That was something Karlsson could understand.

'Well, if she's making cream cake, then she's got to be left in peace. It's dangerous tirritating creepy-crawlies just when they're making cream cakes, because it turns the cream sour . . . and

167

the creepy-crawlies, for that matter!'

And so Miss Crawley's final hours with the Stevenson family turned out to be quite peaceful, just as she'd wished.

Smidge and Karlsson had a nice, peaceful time, too, sitting in front of the fire up in Karlsson's house. Karlsson had flown over to the market and bought some apples.

'And honestly paid for the whole lot, with five öre,' he said. 'I don't want any of those fruit stall women losing out on my account, because I'm the world's most honest Karlsson.'

'Did the fruit stall woman think five öre was enough, then?' asked Smidge.

'I couldn't ask her,' said Karlsson, 'because she'd popped off for a coffee when I was there.'

Karlsson threaded the apples on a length of wire and strung them over the fire to roast.

'The world's best apple roaster, guess who that is,' he said.

'You, Karlsson,' said Smidge.

Then they sprinkled sugar on the apples and sat in front of the fire to eat them as darkness began to fall. It was good to have the fire, Smidge thought, because the weather was turning chillier. You could tell it was autumn.

'I shall have to take a little trip into the countryside and find a farmer to buy some more wood from,' said Karlsson. 'But they're devils for keeping their eyes peeled, and heaven only knows when *they* take their coffee breaks.'

He put two more big birch logs on the fire. 'But I've got to be nice and warm for the winter, or you can count me out, just in case they thought otherwise, those farmers!'

By the time the fire had burnt down, it was dark in Karlsson's little house. Then he lit the oil lamp that hung from the ceiling above the carpentry bench. It spread a warm and cosy glow all over the room, and over all the stuff Karlsson had piled up on the bench.

Smidge asked if he could have a little look through Karlsson's stuff, and Karlsson agreed.

'But you've got to ask me if you can borrow things. Sometimes I'll say yes and sometimes I'll say no . . . but mostly I'll say no, because they're my things, after all, and I want to keep them, or you can count me out!'

And once Smidge had asked enough times, Karlsson let him borrow an old, broken alarm clock to take apart and put back together again.

It was fun, and Smidge couldn't think of a better plaything.

But then Karlsson wanted them to do some carpentry instead.

'That really is the best fun of all, and you can make such nice things,' said Karlsson. 'Or I can, at any rate.'

He chucked all the stuff off the carpentry bench and rummaged out some boards and blocks of wood he kept under the settee. Then Karlsson and Smidge set the room singing as they planed and hammered and nailed for dear life.

Smidge nailed together two chunks of board and made a steamboat. He put a little block of wood on top for a funnel. It was a really great boat.

Karlsson said he was going to make a nesting box and put it up under the eaves of his house for little birds to live in. But it didn't turn out altogether like a nesting box, more like a something else that you couldn't quite put a name to.

'What is it?' asked Smidge.

Karlsson put his head on one side and looked at what he'd made.

'It's . . . a whatsit,' he said. 'A really first-rate little whatsit. Guess who's the world's best whatsit maker.'

'You, Karlsson,' said Smidge.

But it was evening now. Smidge had got to go home and get to bed. He'd got to leave Karlsson and his little room, so homely with all its piles of stuff and its carpentry bench and smoking oil lamp and wood box and open hearth, where the embers of the fire were still glowing warm and bright. It was hard to tear himself away, but he knew he'd be able to come again, after all. Oh, he was so glad Karlsson's house was on *his* roof and nobody else's!

They went out onto the front porch, Karlsson and Smidge. A sky full of stars was stretched out above them. Smidge had never seen so many stars, so big and so close. Well, not close really, of course, because they were millions of miles away, he knew that, but still . . . oh, what a roof of stars Karlsson had on his house, close and far away at the same time.

'What're you gaping at?' said Karlsson. 'I'm

freezing cold . . . are you flying home or not?'

'Yes, please,' said Smidge.

And the next day—what a day that was! First Seb and Sally came home, then Dad, and finally and best of all, Mum. Smidge threw himself into her arms and hugged her. He would never let her leave him again. They all stood round her in a ring, Dad and Seb and Sally and Smidge, and Miss Crawley and Bumble.

'Aren't you exhausted any more?' asked Smidge. 'How did you get better so quickly?'

'I got over it when I read your letter,' said Mum. 'When I heard about you all having "scarlit fever" and being in "kworenteen", I decided it would make me even more poorly if I couldn't come home.'

Miss Crawley shook her head.

'That really wasn't very sensible, Mrs Stevenson. But I can come to help out now and then, if you need me. Now, though,' said Miss Crawley, 'I've got to leave right away, because I'm going to be on TV this evening.'

This came as a big surprise to Mum and Dad and Seb and Sally.

'Really?' said Dad. 'This we must see. Definitely!'

Miss Crawley tossed her head proudly.

'Yes, I hope you will. I hope the whole of Sweden will.'

Then she had to get moving.

'Because I've got to have my hair done and have a bath and a facial and a manicure, and then try out some new arch supports. You have to look smart if you're going to be on TV.'

Sally laughed.

'Arch supports . . . but they won't show on television, will they?'

Miss Crawley gave her a disapproving look.

'Did I say they would? I need some new ones anyway . . . and you feel more confident if you know you're perfect from top to toe. Though ordinary folk may not understand that. But we know, those of us on TV.'

She said a hasty goodbye and hurried out.

'That was Creepy Crawley, then,' said Seb as the door shut behind her.

Smidge nodded thoughtfully.

'I quite liked her,' he said.

She'd made them a lovely big cake, with lots

of cream on top and bits of pineapple inside.

'Let's have it with our coffee this evening while we watch Miss Crawley on television,' said Mum.

So that was what they did. As the thrilling hour approached, Smidge rang for Karlsson. He pulled on the string behind the curtain, giving a single tug, which meant 'Come straight away'.

And Karlsson came. By then the whole family were sitting round the TV, the coffee tray was all ready, and the cream cake was on the table.

'Here we are, me and Karlsson,' said Smidge as they came into the room.

'Here I am,' said Karlsson, throwing himself into the best armchair. 'I hear there's some cream cake on offer here, and not before time. Can I have a bit straight away . . . or rather, a lot!'

'Little ones have to wait their turn,' said Mum. 'And that's my seat, by the way. You and Smidge can sit on the floor at the front, and I'll bring you your cake there.'

Karlsson turned to Smidge.

'Did you hear that? Does she boss you about like that all the time, poor boy?'

Then he smiled contentedly.

'I'm glad she bosses me about too, because it has to be fair, or you can count me out!'

So they sat on the floor in front of the television, Karlsson and Smidge, and ate lots of cake while they were waiting for Miss Crawley.

'Here she comes,' said Dad.

And he was right, there she was! And Mr Peck. He was presenting the programme.

'Creepy Crawley, as large as life,' said Karlsson. 'Whoop, whoop, now we'll have some fun!'

Miss Crawley gave a start. It was almost as if she could hear Karlsson. Or was she just nervous, because she was about to stand in front of the whole of Sweden and demonstrate 'Hilda's Spicy Special?'

'Well now,' said Mr Peck, 'how did you get the idea for this particular spicy stew?'

'Well now,' said Miss Crawley, 'when you've got a sister who can't cook to save her life . . .'

She didn't get any further. Karlsson reached out a podgy little hand and switched off the set.

'Creepy Crawley comes and goes exactly as I want her to,' he said.

But Mum said:

'Switch it back on at once . . . and don't do
that again, or I shall send you out!'

Karlsson nudged Smidge and whispered:

'Can't we do anything in this house any more?'

'Quiet, we're watching Miss Crawley,'
answered Smidge.

'You have to put in plenty of salt and pepper
and curry to make it taste really good,' said
Miss Crawley.

She sprinkled away and the salt and pepper
and curry powder flew everywhere, and once the
Spicy Special was ready, she looked roguishly

out of the screen at them and said:

'Perhaps you'd all like to try it?'

'Not me, thanks,' said Karlsson. 'But if you give me their names and addresses, I'll go and get a couple of those fire-eaters' children for you.'

Then Mr Peck thanked Miss Crawley for coming and showing them how to make her delicious Spicy Special, and that seemed to be the end of the show, but Miss Crawley piped up:

'Well now, could I just say hello to my sister at home in Frey Street?'

Mr Peck looked doubtful.

'Well now . . . I suppose so, if you're quick.'

Then Miss Crawley waved into the camera and said:

'Hello, Frida, how are you? I hope you haven't fallen off your chair.'

'I hope so, too,' said Karlsson, 'because we've had quite enough earthquakes in northern Norrland.'

'What do you mean?' asked Smidge. 'After all, you don't know whether Frida is as solid as Miss Crawley.'

'Oh yes I do,' said Karlsson. 'I've been round to Frey Street a few times for a spot of haunting.'

Then Smidge and Karlsson had some more cream cake and watched a juggler on TV. He could keep five plates in the air at the same time, without dropping a single one. Jugglers were pretty boring, really, thought Smidge, but Karlsson sat there transfixed, so Smidge was happy. Everything was good at the moment, and it was just great having everybody there, Mum and Dad and Seb and Sally and Bumble . . . and Karlsson, of course.

Once the cake was all gone, Karlsson picked up the elegant cake plate. He carefully licked it clean. Then he threw it up in the air like the juggler had done with *his* plates. 'Fair enough,' he said, 'that bloke on the TV wasn't bad at all. But guess who's the world's best plate thrower?'

He threw the plate so high it almost hit the ceiling, and Smidge's heart sank.

'No, Karlsson . . . stop it!'

Mum and the others were watching a dancer on the screen and didn't notice what Karlsson was up to. And Smidge staying 'Stop it' didn't help. Karlsson casually carried on throwing.

'Nice cake plate you've got, by the way,' said Karlsson, hurling it up to the ceiling. 'Or *had*, I should say,' he said, as he bent down to pick up the pieces. 'Oh well, it's a mere trifle . . . '

But Mum had heard the crash as the plate smashed. She gave Karlsson a smart wallop on the backside and said:

'That was my best cake plate and not a mere trifle.'

Smidge didn't like Mum doing that to the world's best plate thrower, but he did realize she was upset about her plate, and he wasted no time in comforting her.

'I'll get the money out of my piggy bank and buy you a new plate.'

But then, Karlsson stuffed his hand in his pocket and fished out a little five öre piece, which he gave to Mum.

'I pay for my breakages myself. Here you are! My pleasure! Buy a plate and keep the change.'

'Well thanks, Karlsson,' said Mum.

Karlsson nodded and looked pleased with himself.

'Or buy a couple of cheap vases with it, then you can throw them at me if I happen to come along and you happen to get cross.'

Smidge cuddled closer to Mum.

'You're not cross with Karlsson, are you, Mum?'

Then Mum patted Karlsson and Smidge and said she wasn't really.

After that it was time for Karlsson to say goodbye.

'Heysan hopsan. I've got to get home now, or I'll be late for my evening meal.'

'What are you having?' asked Smidge.

'Karlsson on the Roof's Spicy Special,' said Karlsson. 'But not that rat poison Creepy Crawley makes, believe me! The world's best spicy specializer, guess who that is?'

'You, Karlsson,' said Smidge.

Later, Smidge was in bed, with Bumble in the basket beside him. They'd all been in to say goodnight. Smidge was getting sleepy. But he lay there thinking about Karlsson and wondering what he was doing now. Maybe he was doing a bit of carpentry, making a nesting box or something.

Tomorrow, when I get home from school, thought Smidge, I shall ring Karlsson and ask him if I can come up and do a bit more carpentry, too.

It was so useful that Karlsson had rigged up

the ingenious bell system, thought Smidge.

I could ring him now, if I wanted, Smidge realized, and it suddenly seemed a very good idea.

He jumped out of bed, ran on bare feet over to the window and tugged the string. Three times. That was the signal for: 'Just imagine there being somebody in the world as handsome and perfectly plump and brave and great in every way as you, Karlsson!'

Smidge lingered by the window, not because he was expecting an answer, but he just stood there anyway. And Karlsson *did* come.

'Yes, just imagine that,' he said.

Not a word more. Then he flew back up to his little green house on the roof.

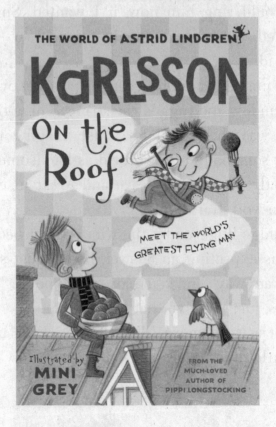

Ever since Karlsson flew in through Smidge's window, they've been firm friends; even though Karlsson gets Smidge into trouble sometimes!

Zoom through their adventures with them as they fly over rooftops, play pranks, tackle robbers, and put on the world's best magic show.

The paper is offering a reward to whoever can catch the mysterious flying object spotted over the city rooftops. Will the world finally discover Karlsson, or can Smidge protect his friend?

ABOUT THE AUTHOR

Astrid Lindgren was born in 1907, and grew up at a farm called Näs in the south of Sweden. Her first book was published in 1944, followed a year later by *Pippi Longstocking*. She wrote 34 chapter books and 41 picture books, that all together have sold 165 million copies worldwide. Her books have been translated into 107 different languages and according to UNESCO's annual list, she is the 18th most translated author in the world.

She created stories about Pippi, a free-spirited, red-haired girl to entertain her daughter, Karin, who was ill with pneumonia. The girl's name 'Pippi Longstocking' was in fact invented by Karin. Astrid Lindgren once commented about her work, 'I write to amuse the child within me, and can only hope that other children may have some fun that way, too.'

For more information visit **www.astridlindgren.com**